CLOSE
YOUR
EYES

ALSO BY NICCI CLOKE

Follow Me Back

CLOSE YOUR EYES

NICCI CLOKE

HOT
KEY
BOOKS

First published in Great Britain in 2017 by
HOT KEY BOOKS
80–81 Wimpole St, London W1G 9RE
www.hotkeybooks.com

A CIP catalogue record for this book is available from the British Library.

ISBN: 978-1-4714-0621-8
also available as an ebook

1

This book is typeset using Atomik ePublisher
Printed and bound by Clays Ltd, St Ives Plc

Hot Key Books is an imprint of Bonnier Zaffre Ltd,
a Bonnier Publishing company
www.bonnierpublishing.com

Transcript of 999 call: 15th May, 2015, 10.28 a.m.

OPERATOR: 999, Emergency Services – which service do you require?

CALLER: I – Police, ambulance – help, please [sobs]

OPERATOR: Ma'am, what is the nature of your emergency?

CALLER: He shot them! [inaudible]

OPERATOR: There's been a shooting? Ma'am, what is your location?

CALLER: Southfield High School

OPERATOR: There's been a shooting at the school?

CALLER: Yes, yes, a student – students – oh my God . . .

1

OPERATOR: Okay, stay calm, I'm sending officers to you. What's your name?

CALLER: Julie Wu.

OPERATOR: Are you a teacher at Southfield?

CALLER: Yes, I'm [shouting in background; inaudible]

OPERATOR: Julie, how many people have been shot?

CALLER: I don't know – I can't see – [banging in background; screams]

OPERATOR: Julie? Are you still there?

CALLER: . . .

OPERATOR: Julie, I need you to talk to me. Officers will be with you as soon as they can, okay?

CALLER [whispering]: They found me. I think they found me.

Call terminated at 10:31

Extract from website of Bridgington Evening News, *article published 15th May, 2015, 10.55 a.m.*

There has been an incident at Southfield High School. Emergency services arrived at the school at a little after 10:30 a.m., after reports of a hostile situation on the premises.

One witness claimed to have heard gunfire: 'There was a loud bang, followed by several more. It was definitely a gun.'

Roads are currently closed in the area. A police spokesperson was not available for comment.

More on this story as we have it.

Transcript of radio news broadcast on local station, Treasure FM, 15th May, 2015, 10.48 a.m.

. . . we're hearing that there's a possible hostage situation over at Southfield School after reports of gunfire on the premises. Afia Ahmed from our news team is in the area.

'Hi James, yes, it's just been confirmed by local police that there *is* a gun inside the school, and that one or more students are threatening to use it. There's a police cordon round the area so I don't have much more information than that, but it's a very distressing time here as you can imagine.'

'Absolutely, yes, Afia – this is really shocking news. I'm sure we've got a lot of listeners out there who have children at Southfield – have police provided a hotline for them?'

'Not yet, no, but the advice right now is to stay at home and stay calm. Police say they're in control of the situation and that expert hostage negotiators are already on the scene.'

'And what about the reports of shots already fired? Have people been injured?'

[sirens heard; reply not audible]

'Afia? You still with us?'

'Sorry, yes, James. I'm afraid I don't currently have any information about that.'

IN THE DAYS after it happens, the stories will start to be gathered.

It's a small town, and the community will struggle to heal itself, to accept what has happened. To accept that one of their children has killed many others.

Streets which they have all grown up on are suddenly filled with strangers: with journalists, with police officers, with people who just want to come and *have a look*. Because now the town is famous – for a horrible, terrible reason.

And so the stories are gathered. Because the people of the town (and the people outside the town – people all across the country who watched the news unfold on twenty-four-hour channels, horrified) want to know why, they want to understand why anyone would take a gun to their classmates, how anyone could.

Everyone has an opinion. Everyone decides they know a victim, everyone decides they know the perpetrator. Everyone wants to tell everyone else *why*.

And so the stories are told.

Facebook conversation between Gemma Morris and Remy Dixon, 15th May, 2015, 5.36 p.m.

Gemma: u ok?
Remy: idk
Remy: fukin hell
Gemma: i know
Remy: what they ask u?
Gemma: everything
Remy: me too
Gemma: i can't believe it happened
Gemma: i can't believe he's gone
Remy: i know
Remy: fuked up
Gemma: gotta go, mum's home
Remy: Gem
Remy: you can't ever tell
Gemma: i know
Gemma: i won't

Interview with Aisha Kapoor, 28th September, 2016

When did I meet him? Elijah? Oh wow, I don't know, I guess it was probably the first day he arrived at school. He started late, you know that, right? He joined like halfway through Year 10. I think at the time I felt sorry for him, because it wasn't easy being the new kid at our school. I think I thought, like, *Why would someone do that to their kid?* But then obviously later I found out about what happened to his sister, and why him and his mum had to move away, and then it all made sense. But yeah, at the time, I felt a bit sorry for him. But it wasn't like I paid him a lot of attention apart from that, really.

Yeah, I mean, he seemed okay – he was in my form so we had a lot of lessons together. He was pretty quiet, he never said much in class or anything. Gemma always used to say he was hot but I didn't get it. I kind of thought he was creepy at first to be honest. He stared a lot. He drew on his hands a lot too, I always remember that. Like, real fiddly, detailed stuff, like proper tattoos. Art was his thing – you probably already heard that, right? That was when people really started to notice him, because the stuff he did, it could be really beautiful. Different, you know? I remember this one time, we were supposed to be painting this stupid fruit bowl that Mr Conrad had set up for us. It was, like, really boring but we had all the paints out and the easels so everyone was just kind of messing about and flicking paint at each other or trying to mess up each other's pictures – hey, could I get some of that water?

What was I saying? Oh right, the art thing. Yeah, everyone just messed about and nobody actually had anything worth looking at really. Well, except for all the geeks obviously, they'd all drawn in all the fruit all perfect you know, like, of course. Mr Conrad was pretty annoyed going round looking at what we'd all done, but when he got to Elijah, his face went all weird. He put his hand up to his mouth, kind of like this, and he just kept it pressed there while he stared at the painting like a total weirdo.

So obviously we all went over there to have a look too, and it was totally sick. Like, in the good way and the bad. There was colour swirled everywhere, so it took you a while to really focus on the fruit, to realise how gross it was. He'd painted them all exactly in their right position, but all old and rotten, green and mouldy, you know, with maggots and flies and stuff. It was so disgusting, and nobody really knew what to say. I think we all just stared at it until the bell went. It was *so* weird.

But yeah, we got to know him, I can't really remember how, I think Gemma started flirting with him on a trip once actually, that was probably it. So then we invited him to sit with us one time at lunch. And actually, he was a pretty funny guy once you got him talking. Like, quick, you know? Always with a funny comeback or picking up on something stupid someone had said. Like my brother. Ash really liked him, he thought he was cool. So then we started hanging out with him at lunch, and then, after a bit, after school. Just normal stuff, you know, like the skate park or town or whatever. We'd just sit and chat, same as we always did. By the time we finished Year 10, he was hanging out with us at weekends as well. We'd go get chips and sit by the river on a Saturday afternoon, that kind of thing. He was always super quiet but most of the time, if we invited him someplace, he'd go.

I think he liked all of us, yeah. I mean, he always got on especially well with Elise, but I guess that was cos she was new too, she only started in Year 9. He always seemed a bit scared of Gem but that was pretty normal, I guess, most boys were scared of Gem. He and Ash were always close, they just got each other.

By the time we started Year 11, he was part of the group, we saw him all the time. To be honest, it felt

9

like it had been us six for ever, I couldn't remember what it was like before. He was one of us, you know? We were a *group*. We even went on holiday in the February half-term together, did you know that? To Newquay, even though it was cold. That was really good, it was the best. I laughed so much.

Sorry, I—

It's just . . . Remembering, you know. I just—

Yeah. A break would be good, thank you.

THERE ARE SIX of them, by the sea.

The twins, Aisha and Ash. She's laughing, her head thrown back, her flip-flops held in her hand. But Ash is standing quietly a little way from the rest, staring out to sea while the waves foam up into nothing, lacing round his feet.

Then Gemma, her T-shirt shoved in her handbag, pink bikini glowing against her skin. The weak winter sun is setting behind her as she stretches a hand up to take a selfie, the dying light making her blonde hair glow. And Elise, taking a photo too – of her name spelled out in the sand, the water creeping closer. Gemma loops her arm through hers and they walk on, heads held close together.

Remy: skimming stones across the waves, a beer held loosely in the other hand. He's getting ready to turn and splash one of them, Ash or Gemma, he hasn't decided yet.

And then Elijah, walking quickly across the sand, spraying it up with each step. He has a carrier bag in his hand; because he's the tallest, he often has to go and buy beers for the group. He makes his way towards Ash, as he usually does. They stand together in silence and watch as the sun drops down to meet the sea.

* * *

Later, back at the campsite, they sit around a foil barbeque, which isn't allowed. Ash was the only one who thought to bring tongs and cutlery (but then, Ash is the only one who thought to bring toothpaste, and an extra towel, and torches – that's kind of Ash's role in the group). But Elijah brought the meat; his mum's current boyfriend works at the butcher's and brought home a load of leftovers last night which Elijah promptly stole. So Aisha and Gemma sit by the barbeque, turning sausages with forks and trying not to drop them, while the others slouch around outside the tents and listen to music playing from Remy's portable speakers.

They all remember this evening differently, later. Elise will think of the way they laughed, the way the laughing seemed to go on forever, until she felt as if she was floating on it, up and away. Remy, though, will remember being drunk, and restless – he will remember them bickering: Ash and Aisha, Gemma and himself.

But they will all remember that the stars were out, the sky studded with them, and that they lay back against rucksacks and sleeping bags, the last smoke from the barbeque curling up above them.

'I don't want to go back to school,' Aisha says, reaching out to take another handful of Haribo. 'Hey, when we finish our exams, can we all go on holiday? Like, actually go *away* away?'

'Yes!' Remy rolls onto his side, grins at them. 'Maga!'

'Urgh,' Elise says, shaking her head so that her dark hair spills out over the rolled-up hoody she's leaning on. 'I'm not going to Magaluf. Let's go somewhere proper, somewhere real. Like Morocco or Barcelona or something.'

'Somewhere *proper*,' Remy says, mocking her, but he doesn't argue. Elise is the only one he never argues with.

'I'm up for Maga,' Gemma says quickly. She glances sideways at Remy but he's lost interest, looking at something on his phone.

'There's no chance our parents would let us go to Maga,' Ash says. 'But we could totally all go to Spain. Our aunt has a house out there.'

Elijah is quiet. But Elijah is always quiet. That's kind of *Elijah's* role in the group – he listens, he thinks, he makes the occasional sarcastic comment that can make them all crease up laughing.

And every so often, he takes the lead. And *they* listen to him.

So when he sits up after a while, and says, 'Let's go down to the sea', they do.

Aisha watches him as they all make their way down the rocky footpath. She sees the way his dark hair falls in a swoop across his forehead, often slipping down to hide an eye, a cheek. She's noticed how, when he's around the five of them, he's quicker to push it back. At school, often, he still hunches over his desk and lets it curtain him away from the world. She knows that some of the kids at school still call him 'weird' or 'freak' but she likes his quietness, she doesn't find it strange. As they reach the sand, she thinks – maybe she's a little bit drunk – how he's completed their group. She links her arm through Gemma's and grabs a fistful of marshmallows from Ash with the other hand.

'Gonna rain,' Remy says, and the second he does the first fat drops start falling on the sand.

'Who cares!' Gemma runs ahead as she yells it, arms held out wide. She's a little drunk, a little sugar-high, and she spins around in circles ahead of them, calling back. 'C'mon, losers!'

She is always calling them names. Losers. Geeks. Freaks. Aisha thinks it's funny, affectionate. The others, though, don't always feel that way. Sometimes being called a loser doesn't feel affectionate, no matter whose mouth it's coming from. But just then, it *does* seem funny. They all laugh, they all follow her. If they are losers, they're losers together. And they run through the rain and they're still laughing.

When they reach the water's edge, the rain abruptly stops. A passing cloud. And slowly, as they stand there with the waves shushing around their bare toes, the stars start to reappear above them.

It's Ash who will remember this moment best. He'll remember how the sky suddenly clears, becomes bright even though it's night, and how they are all quiet, even Remy. And how, even though he's the only one who hasn't had a drink, he feels like he should say something. It feels like a special occasion, weirdly, and he wants to tell them all about how unimportant their upcoming exams are, and how the fact that they're all together, right now, in this very, very quiet night with all its stars, is all that counts. All that will ever count.

But that would be lame. So instead he says, 'Wow.'

And Elijah says, 'Yeah.' Because often they are two parts of the same thought.

After a while, Elise takes a step deeper into the shallows, her pale calves swallowed in the moonlight. 'I feel like I could just walk and walk,' she says, and then she laughs. She turns around and looks at them all. 'I'm really glad we came here,' she says. 'This is way more important than revision.' When she says it, it doesn't sound lame.

'Me too!' Gemma splashes in right up to her knees. 'Guys, it's so warm! Come in!'

It isn't warm. It's cold and thick, silt and seaweed and fish slipping past their skin, but they keep going. They wade in, the six of them, right up to their waists, and then they stand and look at the stars again.

Ash, when he remembers, isn't sure if they are all holding hands.

But he knows that, at some point, Elijah's fingers find his. He knows that, with the weight of the sea pulling them back, they hold onto each other.

Often, looking back, that will seem the most important thing to him.

Extract from the private blog of Ashok 'Ash' Kapoor,
15th May, 2015

I don't have the words.

I don't know how to say the things I want to say, or who to say them to.

Why'd you do it, man? How did things get this way; how did we miss it? We should have stopped you, we should have pulled you back from the dark.

We didn't see the dark. We didn't see it closing in on you. We didn't want to see.

And so everything that happened is our fault too.

I'm sorry.

I miss you.

Why?

Interview with Aisha Kapoor, 28th September, 2016

I think about it all the time, that camping trip, because it's like the last proper happy memory, you know? When it was all six of us and everything was still normal and we were all fine. When we got back to school after that, that's when things started changing, I think. That's how it feels now anyway, looking back.

I guess it's just . . . it's a lot of pressure, isn't it? The teachers make you feel like it's the biggest thing you'll ever do, even if nobody actually ever cares about your GCSEs in the real world. And it was fine for Ash and Elise, 'cos they were the smart ones, they knew what they wanted to do, but for the rest of us, we were like, we're sixteen, we don't know what we're going to be doing in five or ten years, you know?

I didn't even know what I was going to do after GCSEs, let alone the actual future! I'd applied to go to the college in town, same as Gem and Remy, but that kind of made me feel sick, because Ash got into the fancy sixth form way over in Kings Lyme. It meant he'd have to get this stupid bus at like 6.30

in the morning, but he didn't mind, Ash always got up early anyway. I don't know, I guess it was just the first time we'd be at different schools, you know? I'd never been apart from him that long. I know that makes me sound really stupid.

No, he wasn't going to be on his own, Elise was going to the college too, like the clever ones together. Although she wasn't excited about it like he was; she kept moaning about the bus and stuff. But Elise never really got excited about anything, that was just how she was.

Huh? Oh. Um. Yeah, maybe. Maybe I was a little bit jealous. But also, I just wasn't excited about college. Gem knew she wanted to do beauty therapy and Rem was just doing it to make his parents happy, because his plan was to work with his brother eventually and he didn't need any qualifications for that really – his brother has his own business, on the industrial estate? It's something to do with trainers – insoles I think? For sports? I don't really know. So, anyway, that was them sorted. But my parents kept asking me questions, like *Beta* – that's like dear or hun or whatever, well, actually it literally means 'son' but it's just a nice thing, you know, they always call me that. Anyway, they were always all *Beta, what about business?* and *Beta, are you sure you want to take geography? How about law, no?* Because they'd got it in their heads that I was the business one, that I'd make all the money and Ash would write books and be a professor and that kind

18

of thing. And I was starting to panic, because I didn't know if I *wanted* that, but I didn't have anything I wanted more. I just liked being at school, I liked learning a bit about everything, not having to decide. I wasn't ready for things to change.

Elijah hadn't actually applied to go anywhere, not that I know of anyway. He would talk to Elise about it so I only overheard stuff, but I know he wanted to do tattoos. His mum would've let him, she didn't care *what* he did, she didn't care full stop. But the equipment is all really expensive so he needed to save up. Elise would go through the paper with him looking for jobs. I think she went with him to all the cafes and stuff in town, which was probably a good plan. You know, because Elise was pretty and chatty and stuff, and Elijah was kind of intimidating, if you didn't know him. I don't know, just big and quiet, just kind of there, *watching* you.

No, it didn't work. They kept on trying, Elise sort of pushed Eli to keep trying; she'd keep on printing his CV for him, big piles of them for the two of them to hand out everywhere, but he never got any phone calls from it or anything. Nowhere was hiring, nowhere's ever hiring in our town. Well, I mean, Gem got a job pretty easy but then that's Gemma – she gets what she wants, people don't stand a chance really. And Remy was working too, he was collecting glasses at one of the pubs but that's only because his brother's friend got him the job.

And it started getting warm really early that year, I remember that. After Newquay, it stopped being cold, really, but they just kept the heating on in school anyway, like nobody had really noticed we didn't need it. And loads of our classrooms were on the second floor so the windows don't open properly and everything started to stink. That was what school was like for us then, it was like suffocating.

MONDAY MORNING DAWNS before it feels as though the weekend has even started. Aisha makes her way to school, late, stale-mouthed and sore-eyed, a phone full of messages from Gemma even though the two of them saw each other barely eight hours ago.

The messages are about a boy, and the boy's name is Paul. He isn't really a boy either – he's in his last months of his last year at the community college and he drives a beaten-up old Ford Escort around town at lunchtimes. He met Gemma outside a partied-out house in the early hours of a Saturday morning a month or so ago, and now Sunday nights are all about Paul, because Sunday nights are karaoke nights at the cheesy little club in town – and on Sunday nights that cheesy little club doesn't employ bouncers.

All of the college kids think karaoke is hilarious and lame, they say words like 'ironic' and 'retro' when they talk about it. They show up every Sunday and they laugh and drink and don't seem to mind Aisha and Gemma, squeezed into a corner of their sticky booth, Paul's arm sometimes creeping tantalisingly close to Gemma's shoulder on the back of the vinyl seat.

Aisha doesn't really need to make excuses, because her parents and Ash are all in bed by 10 p.m. most nights, but just in case she told them last night (like she did last Sunday, and the one before that) that she was going to revise at Gemma's (geography, because it's the only subject the two of them are taking on their own). Telling this medium-sized lie makes her stomach turn every time, and it feels worse now, in Monday-morning light. Aisha doesn't like telling lies.

She will if she has to, sure. But she doesn't like it.

She misses registration but makes it in time for first-period English. In this class, the regular GCSE class, it's Gemma, Aisha, Elijah and Remy. Ash and Elise are off in their advanced group. Normally Aisha doesn't care about that; Ash has always been the smart one, the geek. They all tease him about it at home.

But going into English that day, Aisha feels heavy and sad. *I'm the stupid one*, she tells herself, which isn't true. Gemma would tell her that, if only she asked. Except Gemma is too busy looking at Paul's Facebook.

Elijah would tell her, if only she asked. But nobody ever asks Elijah.

The teacher, Mr Richfield, arrives, red-faced and flustered. He's young, much younger than any of their other tutors, and this is his first year teaching. Gemma thinks he's cute; Remy thinks he's prey. He fumbles with his briefcase, pulling out a stack of their essays which immediately cascade to the floor. 'Shit,' he says, and flushes blotchily as they laugh. He stoops to gather the papers and then strides around, returning them to their authors.

Aisha is sitting next to Elijah when his is returned. He swoops it off the desk and into his bag but not before she sees the 'D' circled neatly in red on the front. This is surprising; Elijah is good at English. But she doesn't pay much attention, because hers is delivered next, its own circled red letter a C. Her grades are getting lower and that is not the direction they are supposed to be going.

'Okay.' Mr Richfield is back at the front of the class now, tossing his suit jacket over the back of his chair, where it slowly slides to the floor. Damp stains are starting to form on his shirt and he tugs open the window before going back to the whiteboard. 'So, I hope you all read Chapters 24 and 25 over the weekend.'

Aisha looks at her copy of *Of Mice and Men*. She did not read Chapter 24 or Chapter 25. She didn't read Chapter 23, either.

She leans over to Elijah. 'Did you read it?'

He looks up at her and smiles. 'Yeah. I already read the whole thing last year.'

'Of course you did.' She dips her head and looks at the cover of his copy, dog-eared and battered just like her one. There is something comforting about the smell of the classroom and of him: yellowing pages and a damp greenness, like rivers and wet grass. Elijah always smells wintery and of the outside. Even now, in the heat, his clothes seem to hold some of the cold.

She remembers a time, not so long ago, when they were all at Remy's one afternoon after school. Gemma and Rem lounging in front of the TV, Elise and Ash in the kitchen microwaving popcorn. Aisha was kneeling in front of the iPod dock, flicking through the songs on Remy's phone, when Elijah came up behind her. He was in a good mood that day, even humming along to the song, and his presence behind her was solid and comfortable.

'I don't know what to choose,' she said, sighing, and as she did he reached down and smoothed her loose hair back into a ponytail. It was just for a second, the presence of his fingers feather-light, and then her hair swung back down again, released. He didn't say anything and neither did she, but when she finally chose a song and turned around to see him gone the hairs on the back of her neck stood up.

'Will you tell me what happens later?' she whispers now, as Mr Richfield struggles to interrupt a conversation in the front row.

Elijah looks up at her, already bent over his ink-frilled fingers on the desk. 'Yeah,' he says, his voice soft, 'but it's really sad.'

Later, in the cafe in town, Elise picks up Remy's copy of the book. 'Isn't this amazing?' she asks, spearing some sad-looking lettuce leaves with her plastic fork.

'Yeah, it's all right,' Remy says, surprising everyone.

Aisha picks up a limp chip and nibbles at it. She sees Paul enter the cafe before Gemma does, and her heart sinks; Paul is with a pretty blonde girl who has a hand resting on his elbow as they join the queue for food.

'Easter weekend,' Ash says, 'it's the music festival, right? Are we going?'

Remy rolls his eyes. 'So lame.'

'Not lame!' Gemma says, elbowing him. 'Music and booze in a field, for free! What's lame about that?'

'Please.' Elijah puts down his sandwich. 'It's all Abbots Grey ladies with their picnic blankets and their pre-mixed Pimm's in cans.'

'So you don't want to go?' Ash looks at Elijah, surprised.

'Oh, I want to go.' Elijah picks up his can of Coke, tips his head right back to get the last drops. 'That makes it more fun, right?'

Ash smiles; Aisha puts her chip back down, still unfinished.

'I can talk to my dad,' Elise says. 'Maybe you guys could all stay over?' Elise lives with her dad in a big house on the edge of town, right by the fields where the festival will take place. He's never home, and she's learned not to ask where he's going – that's been part of the deal ever since he agreed she could come and live with him instead of with her mum, two hours away. The other part of the deal is that he never tells her off about going to school with lilac lips or rose-patterned nails, which Aisha eyes enviously. Elise pulls her hair back into a loose ponytail, totally unaware of all the boys – and the girls – who are watching her in the room.

It's always seemed weird to Aisha that Elise still hangs out with the five of them. She could be part of any group she chooses; people are desperate to hang out with her, the popular kids, the smart kids, even the sporty ones, because Elise is the fastest runner in their year. But Elise chose them, chooses them every day. She doesn't even seem to notice the others.

'Sounds fun!' Aisha says, but really she's looking at Gemma, who's just noticed Paul and the blonde girl in the queue, her face frozen like a cartoon.

'Yeah,' Gemma says a second later, blinking and turning to look at Elise, her smile weird and sharp. 'Perfect, Lise. I'll raid the rents' drinks cupboard.'

'Me too.' Remy's attention is waning; his bright blue eyes scan the tables at the back of the room, where a couple of his gymnastics mates are sitting. He pushes a hand through his sandy hair and its styled quiff. 'Yeah, I'll sort us out.'

It's often seemed strange to Aisha that Remy stays around too. At least with Elise, there are connections; she's close to Ash on account of them both being geniuses, close to Gemma on account of them both being beautiful. But Remy's connecting lines are harder to trace. He has been friends with the twins since they were at junior school, though Aisha doesn't think either of them can really claim to be close to him. She can't remember the last time she had a conversation with him, just the two of them. But occasionally he'll surprise her; he'll put his arm round her when he's drunk, call her 'Aish'; he once referred to her as his 'best girl mate'. He and Ash used to be much closer, in the first years of secondary school at least. They both loved computer games, World of Warcraft in particular. But then Remy became cool for his other extra-curricular activities; then his boy's body became a gymnast's – and even Aisha will admit, watching him pull himself slowly up on the parallel bars or the rings, every muscle in his torso taut and alert, that it makes her stomach loop deliciously – and suddenly Remy wasn't around so much any more.

Nowadays, Remy and Ash still seem to find at least one afternoon to spend in Ash's room; though the games they play now are very different: Grand Theft Auto, Halo, Call of

Duty. Sometimes Elijah is there, but more often it's the two of them. Aisha's room is next to Ash's and on these days she'll sit on her bed with the door open, trying to make out the conversation inside. There never seems to be much, though it's a comfortable silence. Two people who are just really used to being with each other, but Aisha doesn't think it goes any deeper than that.

Gemma, she's different. She and Aisha only became friends in Year 8, after they worked on a science project together, but she feels like they know everything about each other. They talk for hours: on the phone, on WhatsApp, on Facebook. They pass notes in class; they sit together at break and at lunch. Gemma has her faults – any of the others will tell you that – but Aisha feels like she's trusted her with things she's never, *could* never, trust anyone else with.

Plus she's really fun; she makes Aisha laugh. She makes Aisha feel bold, powerful. She gives her the confidence to do things she never thought she'd do.

And that's what friends are for, isn't it?

Facebook conversation between Aisha Kapoor and
Gemma Morris, 15th March, 2015, 4.43 p.m.

Gemma: who you think that girl was?
Aisha: at lunch?
Gemma: yh
Gemma: the slutty one lol
Aisha: prob just his friend.
Aisha: waaaay too ugly to be anything more
Gemma: lol
Gemma: yh
Aisha: did he msg you today?
Gemma: no
Gemma: ☹
Aisha: playing hard to get lol
Aisha: he was so into you last night
Gemma: ikr
Gemma: lol
Gemma: r u free Fri night? there's a party at some
guy's house, we could totally crash
Aisha: yeah sure!
Gemma: you can borrow my blue dress if you want

Aisha: ahhh thanks

Aisha: hey, u think elise is into ash?

Gemma: LOL

Gemma: no

Gemma: do you?

Aisha: I dunno

Aisha: maybe

Gemma: no I think they're just mates

Gemma: geeks together lol

Aisha: lol yeah

Aisha: i can't do this stupid geography homework

Gemma: ikr

Gemma: I feel like we prob missed something important last week

Gemma: bunking is naughty lol

Aisha: haha

Aisha: you'll have to flirt with sexy steve to get the answers

Gemma: ooooooh yeah steve

Gemma: with his trousers up to his armpits

Gemma: soooo hot

Aisha: lol

Aisha: music festival on sat will be cool

Gemma: yh I think so

Gemma: I mean

Gemma: it'll be lame

Gemma: but we'll all have fun

Aisha: yh

Aisha: can't wait x

Interview with Aisha Kapoor, 28th September, 2016

It's really hard, thinking about those few weeks, even just silly stuff, just us joking around. It wasn't even that long ago and we were just doing stuff like any other group of friends. And now everything is ruined – now I have to read about us all in the papers and in magazines and I have to see people talking about us on TV shows, where they go over everything and they analyse us and stuff. It's horrible. I feel like I want to scream. Because they get it all wrong. They don't understand. They make us all out to be totally different to how we are. Were, I mean. Especially Elijah. Elijah wasn't how they make him out to be.

No, the music festival was totally different. They use it as an example, you know; they say that it should have been obvious then. But it wasn't like that. It totally wasn't like that.

So we'd been out the night before, just me and Gem. That was kind of what started it, I guess, because Gemma had been seeing this guy Paul, who was two

30

years above us, he was at college. Well, not *seeing* really, not officially or anything, they just hooked up a couple of times but they really liked each other for sure. So that was kind of the reason we went to this party at some other guy's house, so Gemma could hook up with Paul.

But actually when we got there, Paul wasn't there, not at first. And we knew a couple of the other guys, from this bar in town we sometimes went to – oh my God, am I going to get in trouble for telling you that? Can you leave that bit out?

Yeah, so we were just kind of hanging out in one of the bedrooms, kind of messing around on this guy's computer, listening to music and stuff, when Paul finally turns up. He was really drunk but then I guess most people were by then. He was all over Gem which wasn't how it usually was, he was normally more secretive about it in front of his friends, even though obviously they all knew. But that night he was kissing her and pulling her on his lap and he didn't care. He kept on spilling his drink and laughing at stupid stuff and all his friends were teasing him for being so drunk but he was kind of cute really. After a bit him and Gemma went off to a different bedroom but I was fine. I just hung out with his friends, they were nice. I don't mind talking to new people really, or I didn't then, anyway. Some of the girls were a bit funny about us being younger. I heard a few bitchy comments about Gem and Paul but that was it, everyone else was really cool and made sure I wasn't left out. So I didn't mind.

Gem came back after a bit and she was really happy, all giggly and we stayed at the party for a little while and then when it started getting quieter we left. I stayed over at Gem's because it was a Friday, and we stayed up late talking and laughing in bed. It was so fun. It was just another girly sleepover, you know? We were just talking about boys and stuff.

So she didn't even go home with Paul, that's the thing. They were texting and stuff . . . but yeah, nothing serious. Nothing to deserve . . . that.

IT'S ANOTHER UNSEASONABLY warm day, that much is true, but there are clouds moving swiftly across the sky and the smell of rain is everywhere. They've found themselves a spot off to one side of the field, close to the trees that run along the edge, where they've still got a good view of the stage. Ash brought his parents' picnic blanket, and Elise has spread her oversized scarf out beside it, so there's just enough space for them all to sit down, the grass still slightly spring-damp. They listen to a terrible Year 10 band play and they drink from the two-litre bottle of vodka and Coke that Elise has mixed up.

Elise herself is quiet, laying back on the scarf with her hair fanning across the fabric in inky twists, her bare feet with their purple toenails buried in the grass. Aisha sits cross-legged and plays with the hem of her dress, her leggings already speckled with grass.

'Told you it'd be lame,' Remy says from his spot, where he's stretched out on his side, head propped up on one hand. His trainers twitch the beat to the music and he grins.

'Here, drink more of this,' Gemma says, pushing the half-empty bottle at him.

'So come on,' Remy says, between swigs, swiping a trickle of vodka and Coke from his chin. 'Who's gonna pull tonight? Ashy boy? Bet you've got your eye on someone.'

He's joking; at least Aisha assumes he is. She's never seen Ash look at a girl as anything other than a person to talk to, or a person passing, or a person who's just a person. But then maybe those are the things Ash and Remy talk about while they're playing computer games in Ash's room, side by side with their eyes on the screen, their thoughts elsewhere. Maybe she doesn't know all there is to know about her twin after all. Maybe they are both changing.

Ash raises an eyebrow at Remy and just laughs, that same old Ash laugh. 'I'm just here for the music,' he says.

'Course you are,' Remy says. 'Eli? What about you? Looking for a laydeeeee?'

Elijah blushes, as he often does when Remy talks to him, leaning down to fiddle with a long stem of grass so that his hair falls between them. 'Fuck off.' The words are soft, they flutter helplessly away on the last, lazy breeze.

'Who are *you* trying to pull?' Gemma asks, plucking a handful of grass and tossing it in Remy's direction.

He laughs. 'I'm just here for the pleasure of your company, guys. Oooh look, new band.'

They're a band who are supposed to be for the parents; who *are* parents, maybe even (in the drummer's case) grandparents. They set up on the stage, in their shapeless blue jeans and their plain T-shirts, and the other teenagers in the audience start looking at their phones, disappearing in the direction of the toilets or the bar or the woods at the bottom of the field where bad things and good things happen.

'Urgh, boring,' Gemma says, rolling her eyes, but Elise says, 'Shhh. Listen.'

And when they start to play there is something good, something they can't really explain. The songs are old and the singer's voice is strained and stretched but still, the music makes them smile. It makes Aisha think of car journeys with her parents; it makes Gemma think of a family party when she was tiny. Remy starts to sing along to a song they all recognise, 'Brown-Eyed Girl', and when he jumps to his feet and pulls Aisha with him, she lets him. They dance around the others, singing to each other, and then Aisha pulls Gemma up too, and somehow the others follow and the rest becomes a blur.

They dance together on their corner of the field. They dance in front of the stage, not caring who's watching. They dance even though the songs are songs their parents would dance to, and they twirl each other round, stumbling in the grass. Elijah is sent off to the bar, because as always his height gives him the best chance of being served.

When they remember it the next day, nobody will be quite sure how it happened. Remy will say that he was dancing with Aisha, that his back was turned. Ash will say he was pushed out of the way, that he stumbled and fell and by the time he got up everything was already out of control. Only Elise will say she saw it coming, that she saw the figure making its way for Gemma, sure and determined and fast, like a shark breaking upwards for a seal on the surface.

Gemma herself is standing looking up at the stage, smiling at nobody in particular as she sways to the music. The song reminds her of Sunday afternoons, her parents dancing round their tiny kitchen, and even though the evening has cooled considerably, she feels warm right the way through.

And then a hand closes on a fistful of her hair, tugging her backwards, her head snapped up to the sky. The stars loom over her and then she rights herself, pulls herself free. She manages a 'What the—' before the first punch comes, catching her on the cheekbone and making her see stars again.

'Stay away from Paul,' the blonde girl from the cafe says.

Remy, trying to push his way through the crowd to get to them, will say that Gemma looked scary then, that she rose up and looked like someone he would not mess with. But Aisha, a step or two closer, will say that there were tears in her eyes.

'What the fuck's it got to do with you?' Gemma says, folding her arms. Her hands are shaking but she isn't sure that she's scared.

'He's not interested in you, little girl,' the girl from the cafe says. 'Stop texting him, you little freak.'

Aisha and Remy have reached them now, Elise approaching from the other side. The older girl might turn and go, the booze-provoked rage suddenly evaporating, if it wasn't for the way Gemma smirks at her. Her hands are no longer shaking.

'He was *pretty* interested in me last night,' she says. 'At James's house.'

The older girl's friends have also arrived, a group of girls with plastic pint glasses in hand, collars turned up against the breeze. 'Oooh,' one of them says. 'Cheeky bitch.'

Gemma smirks again, and she starts to turn away from the group. 'Don't be jealous,' she says to the girl as she does. 'It's *so* unattractive.'

36

This time, the girl gets hold of a clump of Gemma's hair closer to her scalp – and at the same time she aims a kick. Remy is half-laughing, though of course he won't admit it later, and it's Elise who gets there first, who grabs the girl's shoulder and tries to pull her away. It's Elise who takes an elbow in the face, who's knocked backwards onto the grass. It's Elise who one of the girl's friends holds down, who is told, 'You stay down there, darling, where you belong.'

And it's Elise who Remy goes to first – closer, he'll say, though the truth is he thinks Gemma can handle her own mess. And in the confusion that follows it's only Aisha who sees Elijah striding back through the crowd. It's only Aisha who sees Elijah's eyes flashing as he takes in what's happening; Elise on the floor, Gemma's head twisted back by her hair.

It's only Aisha who sees Elijah draw back a fist and send it, without pause, into the face of the blonde girl.

All of them, though, will say they saw her hit the ground.

Facebook conversation between Aisha Kapoor and Gemma Morris, 5th April, 2015, 11.43 a.m.

Aisha: u ok?
Gemma: yeah
Gemma: look at my eye though
[Gemma sends a photo; not retrieved]
Aisha: omg
Aisha: that looks so sore
Gemma: yh it's not really
Gemma: just ugly
Gemma: did u talk to Elise?
Aisha: no but Ash did
Aisha: she's fine
Gemma: Eli?
Aisha: idk
Aisha: I think Ash went out to see him
Gemma: what u think will happen?
Aisha: dunno
Aisha: I think it depends if the girl reports him to the police or school

Gemma: shit
Gemma: I kinda feel bad
Gemma: like, he was protecting me
Gemma: but that was so bad
Aisha: I know
Aisha: I can't believe he did that
Gemma: maybe I should msg him
Aisha: idk
Aisha: I think Ash should talk to him first
Gemma: k
Gemma: did u see tho
Aisha: ?
Gemma: when he ran off last night
Gemma: he was definitely crying

Extract from the private blog of Ashok 'Ash' Kapoor, 6th April, 2015

The days are getting longer and our time together is getting shorter. It seems so strange that soon we won't be going to Southfield every day.

This weekend I was reminded of how much there is to fear in the world outside. It was just a small thing, a small act of violence, but it scared me. I don't think any of us are ready for what's waiting for us out there. We're so used to being safe and together. When that girl attacked G, it was like our little bubble had burst.

E always tells me that we shouldn't be afraid of the world; we should try to change it. That's why things like this weekend scare me – because it seems like sometimes violence is the only answer to violence. The only way to get heard.

ASH GOES ALONE to see Elijah that Sunday, and when he comes back Aisha is waiting for him in his room. His room is always clean and smells of the wood of his bookcases, a new-house smell, and sometimes, in secret, she likes to go and sit there and think. Her room is always caught in the middle – curtains half-drawn, duvet halfway off the bed – and it smells of many things: perfume, hairspray, sleep, often pizza. Things collect on every available surface, school books and half-full mugs of tea crowding up the desk, magazines slipping from the windowsill and the bedside table while clothes creep across the carpet like the tide. It's like her den, but Ash's room is like her church.

'How was he?' she asks, and Ash sits down at his desk and opens the lid of his laptop.

'He was okay,' he says. 'Embarrassed, I think.'

Something about the way he says it makes Aisha think he's not being entirely truthful.

'Well,' she says, testing to see how the words sound, 'I guess he was just sticking up for Gem, right? He did it for the right reasons.'

Ash looks up from his keyboard, his eyes locking on Aisha's. 'Aishu,' he says (only he's allowed to call her this still – their parents are forbidden). 'What he did was wrong.'

41

Aisha nods, relieved. 'Yeah. I know.'

'But it's not his fault.' Ash returns his attention to the screen. 'He doesn't mean to do those things.'

'I know –' Aisha starts to say, but then she stops because she's noticed the plural. 'What things?'

Ash waves his hand in the air, a gesture that's totally copied from his father (and which, today, irritates her in a way it usually doesn't) which means *I hear you, but that's not important*. 'He's got a lot going on,' he says, opening a browser window. 'But look, we should make sure the others are okay about everything. I don't want things to be weird at school tomorrow.'

Aisha looks around at the wooden shelves, the books, the neat white linen on the bed. They feel less calming than they usually do. 'Okay,' she says, despite that feeling. 'So what do I say?'

Ash shakes his head. The window he has open is a forum, Aisha can tell that much from the way it's laid out – a question or a topic in bold across the top, a series of boxes below with a username on the left and a comment on the right – but she's not close enough to read more. She can tell she's losing his attention.

'Just make sure they know he's sorry,' he says. 'Just make sure they're not mad at him.'

And Aisha softens. 'Okay,' she says. She stands to go. 'Are you sure he was all right?'

Ash glances up at her again; he smiles, his glasses crooked on his face. 'Yeah. He will be. It was just . . .' He glances at the floor, searching for the words. 'It was just really terrible. Wasn't it? That someone would just attack Gemma like that?'

It's Aisha's turn to look at the floor (neat navy carpet, hoovered by Ash every Saturday). 'Yeah. Totally messed up. Poor Gem.'

She retreats to her own room and its biscuity jasmine smell. She flops onto the bed, the shiny throw she made her mum buy slithering the last couple of inches to the floor. She thinks about Eli, at home, his hands still bunched into fists. She wonders what the blonde girl's face looks like today, if she has a bruise.

After a while, she turns onto her front and taps Gemma's face in her contacts list. She listens to the rings and she thinks about the way she felt, trapped in the crowd, watching her friend get beaten up.

'Hey, babe.' Gemma speaks in a low voice, like she doesn't want to be overheard.

'You still at your nan's?'

'Mmmhmm.' Aisha can hear the click of a lighter, then her friend exhaling. 'Hiding at the bottom of the garden.'

Aisha laughs, fiddling with the edge of her duvet cover where there's an eyeliner smudge. 'What did they say about your black eye?'

'Dad told them I'd probably fallen over drunk. I couldn't be bothered to explain.'

'Ash went to see Elijah.'

'Oh yeah?' Gemma exhales again, and Aisha imagines her standing in the dark, a plume of smoke rising past the soft fir trees behind her. 'He all right?'

'Ash said he was embarrassed.'

'Well. I dunno. It's . . .' It's not like Gemma to be lost for words; Aisha feels a scrabbling need to provide some for her.

'I guess he did it for the right reasons?' The same sentiment she offered Ash; it goes down equally badly.

43

'I don't think there's ever a *right* reason to hit a girl,' Gemma scoffs. 'Wait, no, that's totally sexist. There's never a right reason to hit anyone?' She takes another drag. 'I mean, that's obviously not true. There's never a right reason to hit someone weaker than you?' She pauses, pleased with herself. 'Yeah, that's probably it. Anyway, it was bad. Him doing that.'

Aisha sighs. 'I know. Are you mad at him?'

'Of course not. He was trying to help me. Aish, the boy is obviously majorly fucked up.'

Something turns in her stomach; a freewheeling feeling, like being on a rollercoaster. 'Ash said . . . I mean, I think . . .' She doesn't know how to put it into words, doesn't know how to express this terrible idea she has that there are things they don't know about Eli, important things.

'Aish, I better go. Dad's calling me. He'll do his nut if he finds me out here.'

'Okay.' The sense of panic gets worse, like something has been unearthed and she needs to bury it again, pretend everything is the same. 'But we're all okay, right? Nobody's mad at Elijah?'

Gemma sighs. 'No, babe. Nobody's mad at Elijah. I'll see you tomorrow, okay?'

After she hangs up, Aisha stays where she is, looking at her phone. She scrolls through her contacts list, looking at her friends' faces. She has them grouped together, to make it easier to call them, to add them all to group messages. **Gang**, she's named the group, and there they all are: Gemma, Remy, Ash, Elise and Elijah.

They'll all be okay, she thinks. She doesn't know what she'd do if they weren't.

Interview with psychologist Ben Matthews, 24th September, 2016

Yes, well, bullying has all kinds of lasting effects. In a case like this, a case where you have evidence of persistent, violent persecution of an individual, there's no telling when a reactive act of violence may come. We've seen studies that show victims of bullying are more than twice as likely to bring a weapon to school than their peers. And that makes sense, of course. In many of those cases, I'm sure the weapons are for self-defence, for security. But then of course there are those who have revenge in mind.

This case has unusual circumstances, in many ways. You have an established group, Aisha, Ash, Remy, Gemma, who welcome a newcomer into their fold. This might encourage feelings of friendship, of *belonging*. But it's difficult to join a group who have been friends for so long, who have their own history, their own language, essentially. In fact, it could make someone feel like even more of an outsider.

This, coupled with the other things happening at Southfield that spring, proved very dangerous. Here we have someone who felt more and more detached from the society around them – and someone who, in the end, felt little guilt or concern about injuring others who were *inside* that society.

Yes, I certainly would describe the events leading up to the shooting as bullying. More than that, I would describe them as triggers. Small factors which contributed to the whole; bricks pulled out until the whole thing came crashing down.

There's only so much one person can take, after all.

Interview with Julie Wu, 23rd September, 2016

Yes, that's correct. I was a science teacher at Southfield for six years. I taught Elijah Edwards when he arrived at the school. I taught all six of them; in fact, the twins and Remy began Year 7 the same year as I joined the school. We started together.

It's not a big school, or at least smaller than the ones I taught at before, so you do get to know the students quite well, especially when you teach them from the beginning, when they are really still children. That makes something like this much harder.

Yes, I became aware of a situation between Elijah and some of the other boys in the class. It was near the beginning of the year, not long after he'd started. It was silly things at first; they'd laugh if he asked a question, call things out sometimes. It was typical teenage boy behaviour, perhaps, though of course that's not any excuse. He did not retaliate and, really, he never seemed to notice much. He was a quiet boy, but he was big, tall for his age and quite broad. No, I did not find him intimidating. Not then.

That incident happened early in April, and it was not an isolated one. There were several fights that week and the atmosphere around the school was tense and strange. It's a stressful time for the Year 11s, of course, with much talk of revision and exams. And it's also an uncertain time, because suddenly they have to begin thinking about the future – and all the excitement and fear that entails. As a teacher you can really see that change during the last term. There's a tension, a kind of hyperactivity, almost a mania. It can be overbearing sometimes.

They were boys from the basketball team – Jake and Derran and Hugo. They were popular boys and they could be disruptive in class but they were not especially difficult to teach. It was last-period biology, which could often be a challenging class – everyone would be tired at the end of the day, and this was a Wednesday too, which is always a low-motivation day for the students. I think they call it Hump Day, don't they?

I was not aware of the rumours, no. I'd been informed by the Head that there was a possible legal issue between one of the boys in Year 11 and a girl from the college, an alleged assault, but we were not informed who. They were still investigating and so the school was careful to keep the details secret. I think they were hoping that it would go away, that the parents wouldn't start to find out. If that had been addressed, perhaps things would not have gotten so out of control later. But no, I had not heard. Not until after that day.

Yes, I suppose I did find him intimidating afterwards.

THE CLASSROOM IS hot and muggy; the air sweet with yeast from a set of Year 7 experiments festering on a shelf. Seagulls wheel over the empty playground; their drying droppings peel on the classroom window. Remy turns his back on the diagram drawn on the whiteboard and grins at Aisha and Gemma on the bench behind him. Elijah is sitting on the end, head bent over his work.

'So we have the trachea,' Miss Wu is saying, but nobody is really listening. Their pens trail across exercise books without forming more than the odd single word. The clock ticks endlessly on.

'Pssst,' Jake says from the bench behind the girls. 'Gem.'

Gemma rolls her eyes as she turns but Aisha can tell she's pleased. There's just the smallest smile at the corners of her mouth, tucked quickly away, and Aisha doesn't understand why. Jake is good-looking (in an *obvious* kind of way, she supposes) and popular, but he's such a *boy*, the kind of boy who thinks it's funny to answer the register with a burp and who regularly says things like 'Aish, guess what?' and then, when everyone waits to hear what he has to say, lets rip with a squeaky fart.

'How wide's *your* throat, Gem?' he asks, and Aisha rolls her eyes. But Gemma just grins and leans closer. 'That depends,' she says. 'How wide does it need to be?'

Aisha shifts in her chair, away from her friend. She doesn't like this side of Gemma; it scares her. It offends her. That someone can act so differently around a certain other kind of person, that they can lose or hide themselves to please other people; she doesn't get it, she doesn't like it. And she knows she does it too and that only makes her madder. She digs her pen deeper into the paper, the ink bleeding over the mehndi design she's been sketching in the margin.

Jake smiles back at Gemma, but he is wrong-footed and she knows it. She turns back to her own exercise book, smiling still, as he fumbles for a comeback.

'Al*veoli*,' Miss Wu is saying to one of the girls near the front. 'Not aioli.' Elijah grunts and turns the page in his notebook. The pages are filling with words, neat, small and impossible to read even from Aisha's vantage point; they remind her of hieroglyphics.

'Hey, Eli*jah*,' Derran says, bored of Jake and Gemma's flirting. 'Guess what? I just made a friend at your old school. Roehawk High, right?'

Elijah's pen drops but he doesn't turn round. He picks it back up and carries on writing and only Aisha can really see how his knuckles turn white.

'Yeah, that's right,' Derran says, voice getting louder as if he doesn't see how Elijah already hears him. 'Some kid in your old form just transferred to St Agnes's. We played them the other week and *guess who* ended up marking him? Chatty guy. He had a whole lot to say about *you*.'

'Bronchi *then* bronchioles,' Miss Wu says, glancing irritably in their direction. 'This is *not* new information, guys. Come on.'

'So,' Derran says, voice lowered again as he pretends to consult notes in the empty pages of his exercise book. 'What's your sister's name? She single? Sounds fun, man, in a psycho kinda way.'

A bolt of real fear hits Aisha then, and even Gemma tenses, remembering the music festival and the calm way Eli drove his fist into someone else's face. But Elijah doesn't move. He carries on writing, even though Miss Wu is too busy trying to help Greg Roscoe find the right page in his mangled textbook to continue the lesson.

'You boys know about Elijah's sister?' Derran says to the rest of his bench, and before he can say anything else Elijah is out of his seat, a hand around Derran's throat. Gemma jumps up to try and pull him away, but Aisha, frozen in her seat, can see how Elijah's knuckles are turning white again, his fingertips digging into Derran's jaw. Gemma's hands *thump-thump* unnoticed against his broad back and the other boys at Derran's bench just stare, half-smiles half-frozen, not quite believing what they're seeing.

'Don't you talk about her—' The words are hissed out, the voice not quite Elijah's but not quite *not* either.

'Elijah Edwards!' Miss Wu storms over. 'What on *Earth*—'

And just like that, the spell is broken. Elijah lets go; for a split-second, Derran's face slumps towards the table-top and then he snaps back up, a smart remark already halfway out. But it's too late, Elijah's turning away – and when Miss Wu tries to stop him, her face stone-cold and furious, he keeps going; he pushes her away.

It's a small push, a half-hearted shove to the shoulder, but Miss Wu is small and slight and she stumbles against the bench behind her. Aisha feels it travel right through her, the thump she makes, but Elijah just keeps on walking. The door shrieks shut behind him but nobody moves. Nobody dares to move.

Later, after dinner, Aisha and Ash are alone in the kitchen. Ash washes, Aisha dries. Their parents are safely propped in the living room, their favourite programme on.

'What do you know about Elijah's old school?' Aisha asks, examining a row of suds on her finger.

Ash leans closer to the pan he's scrubbing: a layer of dirt that just won't come clean. 'What about it?'

'Derran said something in biology today. About his sister.'

Ash frowns, reaches for a swirl of steel wool. 'What did he say?' he asks after a pause.

'I don't know,' Aisha says, watching him carefully. 'He didn't get very far. Elijah went crazy and nearly ripped his head off.'

Ash doesn't say anything, reaching instead for a sponge and resuming his washing. The pan is clean now; Aisha can see that.

'*So*,' she says crossly, poking him. 'Has he said anything to you?'

'I don't know,' Ash says. 'Yeah, there was something.'

'What kind of something?'

Ash sighs. 'Look, his sister did some bad stuff, okay? She had some problems. I don't know all the details. But I know that's why he and his mum moved here – for a fresh start. We need to respect that, Aisha.' He looks at her properly now. 'We're his *friends*.'

He has the desired effect; he shames her.

53

But later, in bed, she begins to feel angry again. Ash has never held anything back from her and now she knows, she can *tell*, that he's keeping secrets. It feels unfamiliar and uncomfortable, an unscratchable itch that crawls through her. She tosses and turns, unable to sleep, and she thinks about getting up and asking him again. The need to know grows and grows, until finally she flips back her covers.

But she won't ask him again. She'll *respect* what he said; she knows he's trying to be a good friend to Elijah, the same way he tries to be a good friend to all of them.

Beside, there's always Google.

You searched for 'Rian Edwards Roehawk High'

About 391,000 results

In the news:

Roehawk Student Arrested
Ryevale Town Crier – Three years ago
. . . the student, named as Rian Edwards, was reported to police after a fellow pupil discovered a notebook filled with 'violent thoughts' and 'explicit descriptions of bodily harm'.

Are video games making our children into criminals?
Daily Mail – 6 months ago
. . . then there's the case of Rian Edwards, the seventeen-year-old from failing state school Roehawk High, who has been under state care after her school exercise books were found to contain vivid descriptions of violence. Edwards was known to be a fan of horror novels and . . .

Rian Edwards (@Rianadon) | Twitter

576 days ago

all of them all of the badness the sickness the smiles the smiles their bad sick smiles

575 days ago

make them pay. they have to pay for what they did for what they do

Facebook | Rian Edwards is a fucking freak!

Bitch went cray cray! lol. Post photos if you have them!

Group has 102 members.

Interview with Classmate A, a former student of Roehawk High, 25th September, 2016

Rian was fucked in the head, end of.

I don't care. I don't feel sorry for her. The girl lost it and she brought it on herself.

All that stuff about her reading horror novels and playing violent computer games and whatever, that's all bullshit. *I* like horror films. *I* like computer games. We all did. You didn't see any of us threatening to kill everyone, did ya? I'm telling you, it was in her the whole time. She was evil. Proper evil. The drugs just brought it out of her.

Well, *yeah*, that was the 'official' diagnosis, but you've seen the papers, right? They all *say* she was evil. I've heard people like you before, making all these excuses, but I ain't interested.

Okay, fine. I'll start at the start.

She was always a bit weird. Bit of a loner. She was smart in lessons though. When we were younger she always got top marks in everything. She'd just sit in the library at lunch, reading or doing extra work. She was a bit of a shadow, to be honest.

Then yeah, I guess she fell in with a bit of a bad crowd, round about Year 9, I think. She'd ended up being quite pretty, basically, and some of the older kids started taking notice of her. I don't know, this is all just gossip, right, but I heard they were into some seriously twisted stuff. Devil worship, that kind of thing. Huh? What kind of evidence do you need? What, you think they had some kind of Facebook group, like 'I heart Satan'? I already told you, it was *in the papers*. How much more proof do you need?

And drugs, well, that's just a fact. Everyone knew that. They were into some real serious stuff, proper tripping all the time.

She got really pale and junkie-looking for a while. You know, lots of spots, kind of on edge. Jumpy, always looking around. I don't know what she was taking exactly. There was an assembly once, it was in the summer, and it got really hot in the hall. The Head was droning on and on about something, right, and we're all getting annoyed and tired and sweating, listening to his scratchy voice buzzing on about being a good citizen or some other crap, and then everyone in the rows in front starts making a fuss. Laughing and stuff, people getting up out of their seats and trying to get away from something.

It was Rian. She'd been sick on the floor, she was totally out of it. One of the teachers led her out and she was just laughing. It was messed up.

Yeah, I guess who can blame her? Her mum was never around, she'd had to bring up her little brother supposedly, she didn't really have any friends. So yeah, someone starts being nice to her, these guys start showing her interest, giving her a chance to have a good time for once. Of course she grabbed it. And it's not like she had anyone to stop her, did she?

So she started coming to school off her face. She'd talk to herself sometimes. No, seriously. You'd see her like leaning against her locker, mumbling to herself, eyes rolling around.

Are you for real? Of course nobody did anything. You ever been to that school? That's nothing. The teachers see shit like that all the time.

And then yeah. One day, someone looked at her wrong, or said something to her, and she lost it. Starts screaming at everyone in the canteen, throwing plates around. Smashing glasses against the wall. She went for the knives, not that they were sharp or anything. Started threatening people. You've seen the videos.

It was only after that that they went through her locker. Supposedly found all this stuff about how she wanted to kill us all. Wanted to set fire to the school, well, I'd have supported her on that one. No, I never actually *saw* them myself. We didn't even hear the whole story at first, they just told us she was being taken to rehab or whatever. But then obviously the papers got hold of it and somehow they got pictures

59

of her diary and the stuff she wrote in it. Apparently one of the teachers sold them to a tabloid. Standard.

So yeah, when I heard about what her brother did, I wasn't surprised. Coming from a family like that, it'd drive anyone to it.

Interview with psychologist Ben Matthews, 24th September, 2016

It's important to remember that Elijah was really close to his sister. She'd looked after him when he was younger and their mother wasn't around much, she'd been the one who'd explained the world to him. She's this filter for him; everything that happens to him, he asks her about, and she is how he understands things. Then this terrible thing happens; Rian starts to lose her grip on what is real and what is right. Who can really know how much of that soaked into Elijah – whether that hatred she began to feel for the world around her rubbed off on him.

And then Rian is taken away. Elijah has to reassess the way he understands the world around him. And he's young enough to do that, young enough to start building a new set of rules for himself, a new scale of who and what is wrong and right. It's hard, it's traumatic, but he can do it. As far as anyone on the outside can see, Elijah adjusts to life at Southfield, life without his sister.

But Rian's influence was lasting on Elijah. He probably always wanted to follow her, to, perversely, feel close to her again. Her words were probably always there, circling in his head, impossible for him to ignore. The tabloids' treatment of Rian – the bending of the truth – can't have helped either. It must have hurt him to read those things.

Well, that's the thing. Families – siblings – are everything to this story. Those relationships are in our DNA – they *are* our DNA. Whether those relationships are positive or negative, they can stay with us. They can *shape* us. Those relationships have shaped this group of friends; they have been at the root of this terrible event.

Family and friends can be the thing that keeps us going, the thing that makes life worthwhile. But then, on the other hand, when you have especially close familial relationships, those attachments can also have a negative effect, particularly in a situation like this one, where you end up with siblings relying totally on each other. There becomes this sense of being two limbs of the same body. So when they feel angry, *you* feel angry. When that person is hurt, *you* hurt.

It can be very hard to escape those feelings.

Interview with Aisha Kapoor, 28th September, 2016

After I found out the truth, I didn't really do anything, to be honest. It was really sad, all that stuff about his sister. I remember just sitting there that night, reading all these stories about her, and it was like something out of a movie. All this stuff about her being a devil worshipper and taking drugs and then those photos of the stuff she wrote in her school books. I watched the video that someone had filmed of her in the canteen, going crazy and throwing stuff at people, and I felt terrible. It was so obvious that she was high or something, that something wasn't right, and then people were commenting on it and laughing like it was a scene out of *Paranormal Activity* or something. I had to turn it off halfway through; I felt like I was doing something so wrong, like I was going behind Elijah's back. I read another of the stories from one of the tabloids, and then I had to close my laptop and I just lay there awake for ages, thinking about all of it.

I felt so guilty after I read about it, I didn't even tell Gem. I knew Ash was right, it was none of our business. And Elijah was our friend. I didn't want to drag up something that would hurt him. I was worried that Derran would bring it up again, or that it'd get round school, but it didn't, not then. I don't know if Derran was just scared of Elijah or if he felt bad or something – maybe he didn't really know anything in the first place, I don't know. He could have just been planning something *really* horrible, that would've been like him. Biding his time, you know? I don't know if he would have just let Elijah get away with embarrassing him like that, especially in front of Jake and Hugo.

Hmm? Sorry. I was just thinking. Wondering . . . you know. All these things that could have happened.

When did it start? Elijah and Elise you mean? To be honest, I don't actually know. I guess I started noticing they were hanging out a lot more around that time. Quite often they'd sort of end up together at lunch or after school, like at the same table as us but not really *with* us, if you know what I mean? Or they'd start saying they couldn't come out at weekends, but they were hanging out just the two of them. I mean, I didn't really think anything of it because Elise was supposed to be helping Eli with maths and with his job hunt, so I just figured they were doing that all those times. And Eli was round at our house all the time too. Ash and him were in his room the whole time. Remy was hardly ever there.

Huh? No, I wasn't jealous, not at all! I was out a lot too, me and Gem, so I was happy that Ash had

Elijah to hang out with. I was happy that Elijah had Ash, especially when I knew everything he'd been through, you know?

So, it was Gem who mentioned it first, Elise and Elijah. She started teasing them about it, calling them the Gruesome Twosome – I dunno, they were into kinda miserable music and stuff, and they were so serious, always talking about books and history and politics all the time. They had these big ideas, all these things to say about how messed up the world was, and all the things that were wrong with people. They got kind of boring to be around, depressing I guess. We were all stressed about exams, so when we were hanging out with each other we just wanted to forget, you know? Just have a good time and relax.

I guess that's when the group started to break up a bit. Not on purpose, obviously. But we pretty much stopped hanging out all together. I mean, Remy always had lots of different friends anyway, and I spent all my time with Gem – she was still hanging out with Paul, so we spent a lot of time with him and his friends.

No, I really don't want to talk about that. I said I wouldn't talk about that, I'm sure I did.

Can we take another break?

THERE'S A CERTAIN wildness in the air in the canteen by Friday lunchtime. All around them, people are planning their weekends. The canteen staff slice doughy pizzas, smiling, planning their own evenings and pretending not to notice the music playing from phones at various tables in the room. Aisha toys with her slice, not feeling especially hungry. She's only half-listening to the conversation around her, keeping an eye on the door in case Derran and Jake come in. She's been doing this all week, waiting for things to kick off again.

But when they don't, when it seems obvious that Derran has gone in to town for lunch or, more likely, is smoking a joint in a car park somewhere, she tries to relax. She tries to forget the things she read about Elijah's sister, tries to tune back into the conversation between Remy and Gemma. Remy isn't actually sitting with them; he's paused on his way to sit with some gymnastics friends, standing over them with his tray in his hand.

'– watch the second episode, for real, Gem. It gets *so* much better.'

'Yeah, okay.' Gemma takes a long swig from her can of Coke. 'I'll give it another shot.'

'What you guys doing this weekend?' Remy pushes a hand through his hair, glancing at the room behind them, and Aisha wonders who it is he wants to look at him.

Gemma looks at Aisha and grins. 'Girls' night tomorrow night. What about you?'

'Helping my brother out all weekend. Extra money, isn't it? Aish, what's the Ash Man doing?'

She puts down her pizza again, still uneaten. 'Revision, I think.'

'Cool.' Remy glances up at his other friends again. 'I'll catch you guys in chemistry, yeah?'

'In a bit, babe.' Gemma has already returned her attention to her phone, her nails clicking over the screen as she taps out a message.

Remy pauses a second longer. 'You all right, Aish?'

She glances up, surprised. 'Huh? Yeah, fine. Just tired.'

'Cool. See ya later, mate.'

As he joins his gym crew, she hears them laughing and talking. She glances down the table, where Elijah and Elise are huddled over a notebook, looking over something. Revising, she supposes, though Elise looks serious, like she's concentrating – and Elise never really needs to concentrate when she's studying. Information just seems to soak into her skin; she can remember facts she hears once forever.

'They didn't even ask to sit with us,' Aisha says, not really realising she's speaking out loud until Gemma looks up.

'Who? Rem and his mates?'

Aisha nods in Elijah and Elise's direction. 'That's weird, isn't it? Do you think they're upset with us?'

'Nah.' Gemma finishes sending her message. 'To be honest, Aish, I think they just think they're a bit better than us.'

'What?'

'Seriously. Haven't you seen the way they look when they're having one of their little chats about Syria or Ebola or whatever? Like we couldn't *possibly* understand.'

Aisha's pretty sure that Gemma thinks Ebola is a country but she doesn't say that.

'Come on,' she says, pushing her plate away and standing up. 'Let's go over there.'

'Why—' Gemma starts, but she follows anyway.

'Hey, guys,' Aisha says, pulling out a chair opposite Elijah. He and Elise both glance up in surprise, and Aisha can't help noticing how Elijah's hand flops down over the notebook protectively.

'All right, Aisha,' he says, not quite meeting her eye. She looks down at the doodles across the back of his hand: an eye, surrounded by words, printed too small to read. They make a tight, complex pattern, like a maze and she wants to run a finger around it, try to find a way out.

'What you guys up to?' Gemma says, leaning on the back of Aisha's chair, not bothering to sit down herself.

Elise's pale blue eyes meet Gemma's narrowed green ones. 'We're just looking over Elijah's history notes.'

Elijah does look at Aisha then and smiles, just a little smile. 'Shame we can't all be as smart as Ash, right?'

Aisha smiles too. 'Tell me about it.' She waits for a second, but neither Elijah or Elise say anything else.

'Okay,' she says, pushing her chair back awkwardly. 'Well, see you in chem, Eli? See you later, Elise.'

They both wave but half-heartedly, already turning back to their conversation.

'I don't know why you bother,' Gemma says, pulling her phone out of her bag as it pings.

'Because we're all meant to be friends,' Aisha replies, annoyed.

'Oh leave them to it,' Gem says. She finishes her text quickly and slips an arm through Aisha's. 'We've got *way* more fun stuff to think about. Like tomorrow night . . .'

Aisha allows herself a smile. 'Yeah. That's true.'

'Paul says it's going to be a really good night. Just a select group of people.'

'Cool.'

Gemma shoots her a sly sideways look. 'Might be your lucky night, babe.'

WhatsApp conversation between Aisha Kapoor and Gemma Morris, 11th April, 2015

Gemma: omg what happened last night???
Gemma: tell me evrything
Aisha: I don't even know
Aisha: I shouldn't have got so drunk
Aisha: Ash would kill me if he found out
Gemma: well he won't!
Gemma: stop worrying babe
Gemma: you had fun right?
Aisha: I guess
Aisha: yeah
Gemma: well then
Gemma: now tell me all about Tom
Aisha: well . . .
Aisha: he was nice
Gemma: zzzzz
Gemma: yeah yeah
Gemma: what happened??
Gemma: did you dooooo it?

Aisha: um
Aisha: yeah
Gemma: OMG!
Gemma: I'm so proud of you!
Aisha: ☺
Gemma: So . . .
Gemma: did he rock your world?
Aisha: lol
Aisha: not exactly
Aisha: it was . . . nice
Gemma: nice is good!
Aisha: don't tell anyone else
Gemma: obvs!
Aisha: g2g
Aisha: dinner
Gemma: see you tomo babe
Gemma: can't wait to hear all about it! Xxx

IT HAPPENED AT another party, a non-party really – drinks in someone's back garden, the atmosphere flat and anticipatory, as if there was something more, something to go on to. Aisha's not sure why she agreed to have a drink. It's not the first time, but usually she's better, usually she doesn't find it hard to say no. Now her memories are patchy and confused, his face muddled up and the things he said vague and dreamlike.

The next time she sees him is at lunchtime, the Tuesday after the Friday night before. She and Gemma are walking through town, heading for the chip shop, and then he's there, standing in the doorway to the hairdressers. He's half-facing away from them, talking to a guy with an apron on. The pale skin at the back of his neck is newly exposed, the hair shorn and shaped where she remembers it longer.

Aisha smiles; stops smiling. Neither feels natural, her face suddenly a stranger's. They are fifteen steps away, ten. Gemma babbles on and on about a party Paul mentioned on Saturday night. Tom, laughing, stops; in slow-motion, she watches him start to turn.

She remembers how the night began. Gemma sitting on Paul's lap, his hand half-tucked into the waistband of her jeans.

The edge of her bra inching out of her top. Aisha remembers reaching for the bottle again as they started kissing. She remembers Tom sitting down beside her, his warm brown eyes.

She isn't sure how it happened. Time concertinaed together and suddenly it was dark, suddenly they were holding hands.

They are five steps away now, and Tom's eyes meet hers.

She isn't sure how it happened. Suddenly they were holding hands, and drinks were being poured. Suddenly they were face to face on a narrow single bed, a poster of Dora the Explorer beaming down at them. She remembers his breath, hot and malted, on her face. She remembers the way his hands ran hesitantly over her skin, the way he laughed nervously, apologised constantly.

He smiles now, awkward again, and then he turns away. They pass him and then they are crossing the street, the chip shop up ahead.

'Anyway, I was thinking, what if I dyed my hair? Like, Elise's colour maybe? Or maybe not *as* dark, maybe a bit redder?' Gemma hasn't even noticed that anything has happened; Aisha is patiently waiting for her heart to start beating again.

'Yeah, sure,' she says, resisting the urge to rub her chest. 'That'd look *amazing*.'

Gemma doesn't dye her hair dark. She goes blonder still; blonder than the blonde girl from the cafe whose name is Rachel and who Paul still hangs out with. Gemma sees pictures of them together on Facebook all the time. Rachel still has faint bruising around her eyes but her nose wasn't broken and the police have not pressed charges against Elijah. Gemma now happily tells the story round school, casting herself as the victim and Elijah as the hero, but Aisha feels uncomfortable, she doesn't like to remember. She doesn't want to say *that isn't how it happened* or *what he did was wrong* even though those are the things she's always thinking. She tells herself that she's supposed to be his friend, and she tells herself that he's been through some bad stuff. The others have forgotten it; she should too.

The parties go on; the girls go to parties. They stop inviting Elise because Elise always says no. So Aisha spends the parties sitting next to Gemma while Gemma kisses Paul.

But she does, occasionally, get talking to some of Paul's friends. Not Tom; for one, two, three weeks there's no sign of Tom. But to some of the others. Mike, Jamal, Kiera. Other people who call her Aish, who put their arms round her. She starts to feel like a part of the group; she starts to feel funny, smart. When they're sitting around, drinks in hand, people laugh at the jokes she tells, they listen to her stories. She isn't 'one of the twins'; she's just Aish.

And she kind of likes that.

But one night, a Sunday night, she creeps in after midnight and finds a light still on in the kitchen. She freezes in the hallway. If it's her mother or father, she's doomed. She isn't drunk but she's had a drink; she's sat in fat pools of smoke from other people's cigarettes. But then she hears the soft notes of a saxophone. Jazz.

She opens the kitchen door. Ash, sitting at the table with a mug of tea, revision notes spread out in front of him. He looks at her, eyebrows raised.

74

'What are you doing up?' she asks.

'Waiting for you.' He gestures towards the empty cup opposite him, the pot of tea. Only Ash makes tea in a pot. Like the jazz, it's learned and loved from time spent with their grandparents.

'Oh.' She drops onto the bench, pours herself a cup with a trembling hand. She feels tired, so tired. She feels as though she hasn't slept for weeks. 'Sorry. I should've said I was going out.'

'It's okay. Mum and Dad think you went to revise bio.'

'Cool.'

'So, where were you?'

Aisha takes a sip of tea. 'I was with Gem.'

'Yeah, but where?'

She could lie, she should lie, but she finds she can't. 'At Club Ice.'

Ash puts down his mug. 'On a Sunday?'

'Karaoke night.' She shrugs.

'You've been drinking.'

'No.'

'Aisha.'

She puts both hands around her mug, trying to draw warmth into them. For days she has felt cold; all the way inside, right through her bones. It's unseasonably warm for April but she sleeps under two duvets. 'Maybe a bit.'

He shakes his head, drains his own tea. 'Okay. I just wanted to check you were okay.'

'You're not going to tell me off?'

'No. I'm not Mum or Dad.' He gives her a reproachful look. 'Just your twin.'

She smiles, takes a sip of tea. 'Sorry.'

'I'm going to bed. I have a revision session before school tomorrow.'

School. She can't imagine getting up in six hours' time. 'Okay,' she says. 'I should go up too.'

He takes their cups to the sink and she slinks away, towards the door. 'Aish,' he says, before she can reach it.

'Yeah?'

'Be careful, okay?'

He turns away before she can ask him what he means.

She lies awake and thinks about it; but not for long. She is so very tired.

**WhatsApp conversation between Aisha Kapoor and
Gemma Morris, 29th April, 2015, 11.15 p.m.**

Gemma: are you ok? Xxxx
Aisha: no!
Gemma: shit
Gemma: what are you going to do?
Aisha: I don't know.
Gemma: you're not going to keep it tho right?
Gemma: Aish, you so can't
Aisha: I know
Aisha: why is this happening to me?
Aisha: I can't deal with it
Gemma: it's ok
Gemma: I'll help you
Gemma: I promise
Aisha: thnk you
Gemma: get some sleep
Gemma: tomorrow we'll get this sorted
Gemma: xxxx

Interview with Gemma Morris, 27th September, 2016

Yeah, of course I said I'd help her. She was my friend. There was no one else she could ask, anyway. Obviously she couldn't tell her parents, and Ash would've lost his shit. It's not like it was a big deal. She was only a couple of weeks gone. I went with her to the first appointment, and to the stupid counselling thing they made her do, and then to the actual proper appointment. She just had to take a pill and then we went back to mine and watched *Harry Potter* all afternoon until she had to go back and take the second one. And that was it. We didn't really talk about it after that. It's not like she regretted it. It's not like she wanted a kid for fuckssake. Okay it wasn't the ideal situation but I just thought it'd be best to get it out of the way, forget it and move on. Maybe that sounds harsh, but I was just looking out for her. I was trying to make things easy for her.

Nope, it definitely wasn't my idea to tell Tom. He was shagging about three different girls. Paul told me that after. He didn't deserve her time. But Aisha's too sweet like that. She said he had a right to know or something. Maybe she was thinking he'd want to look after her or something. Maybe it was just a way to talk to him. If she'd have told me first, I'd have told her to forget all that. But the first thing I know about it, she's calling me up crying, telling me he's told her he doesn't want anything to do with her, that she was a one-night stand. What a grade-A prick. He didn't even offer to go with her or anything. Not that I'd've let him. No chance, babe.

I felt sorry for her; Aish wasn't used to stuff like that. She didn't know what guys are like. Plus he was her first. That really sucked.

So yeah, all that was going on. And then the blog started around that sort of time as well. Well, that's when people started talking about it, anyway. I don't know who saw it first, or how it got round. But soon everyone was on about it. I guess it was because of who it was about – Jake and Derran were pretty popular so obviously everyone was interested in what it had to say about them.

Was it true? I've got no idea. Doesn't really matter does it? Once people were saying something round Southfield, it might as well've been.

From the anonymous blog, 'Truths from Southfield',
posted 30th April, 2015

Our school is full of secrets. Dirty, festering secrets.
We're rotten to the core.

Like the Year 11 basketball star who's fond of
performance-enhancing drugs both on and off
the court.

Like his team mate who cheats his way through
exams. Who once bribed a student teacher to keep
his biology grade high enough to make the team.

Stayed tuned. There are plenty more secrets to share.

GEMMA DOESN'T CARE all that much about the blog when she first sees the link on Facebook. She's far more interested in a set of photos that have been posted to Paul's wall, photos of him in one of the nightclubs in town over the weekend. Far more interested in one in particular – one where Paul has his arm around a pretty red-haired girl. The girl's hand is pressed to Paul's chest, and both of them are smiling. Gemma stares at the photo, at the girl's hand, her fingers making soft creases in Paul's T-shirt. She searches for *Paul's* hand. Is it up high, like how a friend hugs a friend? Or lower? She finds a shadow right down beside the girl's hip and studies it, her stomach looping.

A new chat window opens, interrupting her thoughts. Aisha. *did u see that blog about jake and derran? omg*

Gemma clicks back to her newsfeed, finds the link. She opens the blog post, scans through it.

how u know it's about them? she types.

She reads the post again. There are fifteen boys on the basketball team and besides, the gossip doesn't seem that interesting to her.

everyone's saying its them. Derran is the star player right? he totally looks like he's on steroids anyway, Aisha writes, and Gemma has to admit that this is true. She clicks back to the photo of Paul, losing interest.

At school the next day, lots of people are talking about the blog. No one is exactly sure who saw it first, or where it came from, but nobody really cares. It is the most interesting thing that's happened since Elijah punched a college girl, and everyone is happy.

By lunchtime, there are rumours that the basketball team's lockers have been searched. As Gemma and Aisha walk down the hill after school, they overhear a group of boys from the year below talking about how the whole basketball team might be suspended.

'I don't get it,' Gemma says. 'Who cares enough about school basketball to take drugs for it?'

'Loads of people,' Remy says, appearing between them and throwing an arm over each of their shoulders. 'You do know how much professional players get paid, right? They all start out somewhere. Anyway,' he says, glancing back over his shoulder, 'you've all seen Derran on a night out. If there's a situation that can be "enhanced", he's your man.'

'So it *is* true?' Aisha asks.

Remy winks at her. 'Most rumours are round here, right?'

'What about the cheating stuff?'

'Jake?' He shrugs. 'No idea. He never comes off as stupid in lessons, does he?'

'He doesn't exactly come off as smart,' Gemma says.

Remy elbows her. 'You totally fancy him.'

Gemma rolls her eyes. She knows Remy well enough not to bother biting – most of the time, at least.

'Anyway, ladies,' Remy says, releasing them. 'Gotta run. Gotta date with a horse and she is a tough ride.'

'Urgh,' Aisha says as he walks away. 'He is *such* a pig.'

'Aish, he was talking about the horse at the gym.'

'Still though. It's the way he says it. Not cool.'

Gemma shrugs and slings an arm around her friend's neck, still warm from Remy's skin. 'You okay, babe?'

Aisha stiffens, just a little, but Gemma feels it. She hates that feeling. She hates the idea that keeping this secret between them might make them less close. 'Want to go out later?'

Aisha shakes her head. 'I'm gonna hang out at home and study with Ash.'

'Oh come on. Study at the weekend! Let's go out. I can get us booze.' She sees her friend weaken. 'I think Paul said some of the boys are going to the Legion to play pool.'

Aisha bites her lip. 'I guess I could come out for a bit.'

'Yay!' Gemma lets her arm fall, squeezes Aisha's hand as hers passes. 'Hey, how much you wanna bet poor old Derran is out drowning his sorrows?'

Getting ready that evening, Gemma looks at the blog again. *There are plenty more secrets to share*, it promises, and Gemma is interested in that. She studies her face in the mirror before she applies her make-up – hair scraped back in a band, skin still blotchy from the shower. She looks at her face often; it is also a thing of interest. Not necessarily in a vain way;

if she's feeling especially critical she thinks her features are average at best, her nose a little wide, her eyes a little close together – but she is fascinated by the way she can paint herself a new one, one which suits whichever mood she happens to be in. She likes drawing in her own lines, painting colour wherever she chooses, adding shadow. This face is her armour.

She thinks of Aisha as she sucks in her cheeks and chases the bone line with a bronzer brush. She thinks of the way she seemed to go cold earlier, just for a second, and she worries that Aisha might still be upset about the abortion (or, worst of all, might somehow blame Gemma for the whole thing). But she definitely *seems* okay, making jokes, laughing at things, *not* mentioning Tom aka Twatface so much. So maybe things are okay, maybe they've got through it together. The thought of that makes Gemma happy so she hopes it's true. But then Aisha has always been different to Gemma, always more thoughtful, always seeing things about people that Gemma doesn't. It's one of the things Gemma likes most about her. It's one of the reasons Gemma often worries Aisha might find someone else she'd rather hang around with.

She checks her make-up, left side then right, lips pouted, lips relaxed. Satisfied, she shakes out her hair and goes to the wardrobe to dress, a little reluctantly. The air is thick and still outside, despite it being earliest May, and with shower-damp skin she actually feels like she can breathe. She rakes through the flimsy rack of clothes on their mismatched hangers, looking for something just casual enough. She picks out a dress she stole from her cousin Leanne – *borrowed* she prefers to think, and besides, it looks better on her anyway. It could work for tonight if she wore the right shoes. *Boots*, she thinks, despite the heat. She likes the way boots look with a dress; likes people to never be sure if she's about to kick them or kiss them. She kneels to riffle through the battered sandals and club-stained heels to find her winter shoes.

The boots are at the back of the wardrobe, and next to them is a bashed-up old shoebox covered in stickers. She's going to be late, and she knows what's inside, but still, she can't stop herself reaching out to take it. She holds it on her lap and takes the lid off very carefully, a sacred routine that can't be rushed.

Inside are tickets and photos and letters, the layers built up like the years, items tossed inside every time she clears out her school bag and handbags. She knows that at the bottom she'll find a Cinderella lipbalm, long worn out, that her old friend Chloe bought back from Disneyland when she was ten. Tickets to *Toy Story 3*, when she and Leanne and her Auntie Elsie went to the cinema in town. The napkin from the posh hotel her mum took her to lunch to for her fourteenth birthday, even though they both stole the slippers from the spa too. She doesn't know what made her start saving things, but now it's almost a compulsion. It drives her dad mad – he can't stand clutter, can't bear an undusted shelf, and so Gemma's memories are all safely stowed here, a little museum that only she's allowed to visit. She can hear her parents downstairs now, laughing about something on the TV as they tuck into their pizza and she feels bad, just for a second, that she's turned down their offer to join them yet again.

At the top of the box is a strip of photobooth pictures, a leftover from their camping holiday at Easter. She flips it over and runs a thumb over the gummy gloss finish. Her, Aisha, Ash and Remy, all crammed into the booth, pulling faces at the camera. So strange, really, that the four of them have stayed close, she thinks, looking at Ash's awkward smile and Remy's long, flat tongue hanging out like a dog's, a bottle of beer in his raised hand. Aisha's sweet, good face next to Gemma's shadowed, shaded one. And yet they all look really happy. They make each other happy.

For a second, looking at the pictures, Gemma feels a surge of guilt about Elijah and Elise, the newly formed Gruesome Twosome. They were off getting fish and chips for everyone when the others found this photobooth outside the arcade, and by the time Elijah and Elise got back they'd all got bored and were playing air hockey. They've probably always felt left out, she thinks. It can't be easy being the new ones, having to have the in-jokes and the stupid stories explained all the time.

So she picks up her phone. She finds Elise's number, the thumbnail image of the inked-on designs on her arm – black roses and stars and a line of poetry Gemma doesn't recognise – and she presses 'Call'.

'Hello?' Elise sounds surprised and that brings another wave of guilt.

'Hey. What are you doing tonight?'

Elise hesitates. 'I – well, I kinda –'

'Look.' Gemma puts the photos back in the box, crams the lid back on. 'Aish and me are going out. Between me and you, she kind of needs her friends around her right now. Girl time, you know?'

'Oh.' The surprise is back. 'Yeah, sure. I can be there.'

'Great.' She slides the box back into place, retrieves her boots. 'We're meeting at eight.'

Gemma: moooooorning
Gemma: how u feeling?
Aisha: bleurgh
Aisha: that escalated quickly
Gemma: lol
Gemma: was fun tho
Aisha: yeh
Aisha: u go home with Paul?
Gemma: just for a bit lol
Gemma: school night!
Aisha: haha
Aisha: was nice to see Elise
Gemma: yeh seemed like she had a good time right?
Aisha: totes
Aisha: she was loving it
Gemma: I like her when shes wild like that
Aisha: lol
Aisha: me too

Aisha: think I had a drunken cry to her in the loos tho, ooops

Gemma: lol don't worry she wont mind

Gemma: u going in for maths?

Aisha: yeah

Aisha: have to

Gemma: think im gonna skive off

Gemma: dads not here

Gemma: ill come in at lunch tho. cover for me?

Aisha: yeah sure ☺

Gemma: thanks babe

Gemma: see u in a bit xxxxxxxxxxx

Aisha: have a nice sleep! xxxxxxxxxxxx

Interview with Gemma Morris, 27th September, 2016

Yeah, that was a fun night. You never got Elise out, especially without Eli. Which was a shame, cos when she let loose, she was so cool. So herself, you know? Elise was never one of those girls who turned into someone else around guys. She knew her own mind, right? I guess that's what got her into trouble, but I liked that about her at the time.

After that, things went back to the way they were. Aish and me hanging out with Paul and his friends, the others doing their own thing. We asked Elise to come out like that same weekend, but she said no. She wanted to hang out with Eli. I just thought *Fuck it*. I know a lost cause when I see one. I just thought she was one of those girls who prefers guy company. And I get that. I'm not *like* that, but I get it.

Elijah. He was quieter then – even quieter than normal. I mean, it's not like me and him spent much time together anyway, so I didn't really care. But I know Aish was worried that he wasn't, I dunno, himself. Even Remy started asking why he wasn't turning up to stuff at weekends or why he'd just sit at lunch with his headphones in. I guess Elise and Ash hung out with him one-on-one more but they were always closer to him anyway.

Yeah, a couple more blog posts appeared after that. There was something about one of the popular guys cheating on his girlfriend, and something about one of the girls taking laxatives to lose weight. Who knows if they were true; I mean, who cares, right? But people liked having the gossip. They started getting interested in the blog, wondering who it'd pick on next. I wasn't bothered. I didn't really have any secrets, to be honest. I'm kind of an open book, babe.

Right. Exams were coming up and people were getting pretty stressed out about it all. Ash and Elise were a fucking nightmare at lunch and stuff – hunched over their books, not bothering to talk to the rest of us. But Elijah didn't seem interested any more. He'd just sit there drawing on his arms. Headphones in. He messed around on his phone a lot, even in lessons. Online all the time, who knows what he was looking at.

Yeah, you could say that, babe. Definitely. It *was* like he'd checked out.

GEMMA STARTS TO find herself watching Elijah. Not all the time, just in quiet moments, bored in a lesson or waiting in the queue at lunch. She's always thought of him as painfully shy, like he's too afraid to even make eye contact with people most of the time, but the more she watches – and she's never really bothered to watch at all, all this time – the more she realises that this isn't true. Elijah is always watching too, watching everyone. His hair might fall forward, shielding him from view, but behind it, his eyes flick across the room, taking in the people in it.

It creeps her out to see it.

One afternoon during English, the class are sent to the library to research an essay on Steinbeck. Remy is off with a torn muscle in his neck, a gym injury, and Aisha has been excused for an emergency dentist appointment on a chipped tooth (a tooth she tells everyone she broke on an apple; actually one of Paul's friends was trying to teach her how to open a bottle with her mouth).

Normally in this situation (not that it's ever happened before), Gemma would keep to herself, or maybe buddy up with one of the girly girls who all bunch together in the front row. She and Elijah have never spent any time together, just the two of them. It'd be weird.

But today, she's curious. So she makes a point of walking across the playground with him, asking him about his essay. She chooses the computer terminal next to his. He gives her a bit of a questioning look but he doesn't say anything; he seems relaxed and maybe even happy to have her there.

'I don't even know what I'm going to write,' she says, clicking idly to open a browser window.

'Did you choose a question?' he asks in his soft voice, his big hands already moving over his own keyboard.

She shrugs. 'I guess I kind of liked the one about Curley's wife.'

He looks at her, surprised. 'Really? Most people are doing the one about vulnerable people. That's kind of the point of the novel, you know.'

Gemma shrugs again. 'Yeah. I don't like how she's the only woman and she doesn't even get to have a name. And they act like it's all her fault, when obviously it's George's.'

Elijah doesn't look at her this time, and his hands keep moving across the keys, but she notices how he sits up a little straighter, his expression becoming tighter. 'Why do you think that?' he asks.

'Well, he knows what Lennie's like,' she says, bored of this conversation already. 'He shouldn't have let him be in that situation. He shouldn't have left him with people he could hurt.'

Elijah chews the inside of his lip, clicks on a search result. 'But George does the right thing in the end, doesn't he? He puts Lennie down. He makes sure he can't hurt anybody else.'

'Yeah, better late than never,' Gemma says, trying to open Facebook even though she knows it's blocked on the library computers.

Elijah doesn't reply. Gemma spends a couple of minutes clicking through some photos of Red Nose Day on the school website, looking for any of their group (well, looking for photos of herself or maybe Aisha), and then she pushes her chair back. 'I'm going to look at the books,' she says. 'That's what the library's for, right?'

Truthfully, she's hoping to find someone else to talk to among the shelves; her interest in Elijah is quickly waning.

But once she's in the stacks, she finds herself looking back in his direction. He's not looking around now; his attention is totally focused on the computer in front of him. Gemma moves deeper into the history aisle, hoping to get a better view, but the computer Elijah has chosen is angled towards the back wall; all she can see is a tantalising slice of white on the screen.

'Hey, Gem,' someone says from behind her, and she turns to find Sean, one of the other boys in their class, grinning at her. 'We're all watching *Game of Thrones* on Hina's iPad in the next aisle, want to join?'

When she returns to her desk ten minutes later, Elijah has gone.

Conversation from online gaming forum, 5-star, 5th May, 2015

Please note: 'betas' is a name adopted by frequent users of the message board, thought to refer to the term 'beta male' and used here to describe themselves as inferior or a lower-level of school society. 'Edwards and Bellas' refers derogatorily to the perceived popular kids at school, particularly those interested in mainstream culture.

betaboy
right guys top 5 bitches u want naked photos of

betaboy
our american friend hacked a ton of hollywood pussy

betaboy
beta rising for life!

the_jump
lol no way

whereswilly
yesssssssss bro

whereswilly
bring it on! all of them!

Dx99
nah way. how???

betaboy
kid got skills

truthteller
guys wtf

truthteller
we're sposed to be better than all the edwards

truthteller
I don't want to see any cheap slut's anything

truthteller
we're here to talk about what really matters, right?

betaboy
dude what matters more than j-law's pum pum?

Dx99
^^lol

Dx99
man's gotta point

the_jump
naaah truthteller's right we're better than this

the_jump
this is the place for talking about how to make things better, not fapping over famous fanny

truthteller
thanks @the_jump

truthteller
if you want to see how to take the bellas and the edwards down, you need to check this out. this is what's going down at my school: [link to *Truths from Southfield* blog, redacted]

Dx99
fuckin lol

the_jump
whaaaaaaaaaaaaat. amazing.

Dx 99
that's sick man. your school is a twisted place to be but good on whoever's calling the bitches out

betaboy
haha that is awesome

truthteller
just the beginning, boys. just the beginning.

Interview with psychologist Ben Matthews, 24th September, 2016

Of course, it's perfectly normal to fantasise about things. When we are attracted to someone, we fantasise about being with them. And when we are frustrated or angry in a situation, it's normal to fantasise about or imagine revenge. These thoughts are cleansing, they release tension – simply put, they make us feel better. The problem comes when you have someone who, for whatever reason, finds it less easy to distinguish between fantasy and reality.

Yes, exactly that – someone who feels very isolated in the world they live in might, over time, find it harder to distinguish between fantasy and reality. If you don't have anyone to say, 'Oh that just made me so angry, I felt like ripping his head off' to – and of course we all say such things, and then we laugh, and the tension is released – you *might* start to think you actually *do* feel like ripping someone's head off. The thoughts become stronger, they're not just a way of expressing frustration any more. You start to *believe* them. Do you see?

99

Right. Now, that's an interesting thing, actually. The internet has made things even *more* complicated, emotionally speaking. In many ways, it has given us a broader horizon, an infinite number of people to connect with, and there are many wonderful and lasting friendships built there. It has been a way to reach out, to truly find a place where you *belong*, even when the place you are geographically can't offer you that. But it's also a place where you can express anger, rage, without consequence. You can say 'I felt like ripping his head off' and there are anonymous strangers who might say 'Hey, yeah, do that!' You can go and read about how angry all these other people are about the world and the people in it. How much *other* people are thinking about revenge, fantasising about violence.

Yes, exactly. It can sort of validate your feelings. It can encourage them.

So, slowly, these fantasises begin to take up more and more psychic space. In this case, they're *all* you can think about. Here, they become a cause, an obsession.

What finally takes this beyond the realm of fantasy? What takes it to the next level, to this terrible act of *actual* violence? Well, it might surprise you to know that it's not usually something said online. Usually – and certainly it was the case here – it's something someone does in *the real world* which acts as the final straw.

Look. I don't think I want to talk about that.

You said we didn't have to talk about that.

No, not guilty. How was I supposed to know? None of us knew what would happen. How could we?

Urgh. Nobody ever gets this part right, they don't understand what it was like, how it happened. They make out like we *planned* it. That's totally not fair.

I guess I might as well start at the start. It was a Saturday night, and some girl Rem knew from gymnastics was having a party. It was him, me and the twins – Eli and Elise didn't even reply to the WhatsApp messages.

Yeah, it was the first time Aish and me had been out with the boys for ages, and we had a really good time hanging out at Remy's before the party. That's what I always remember now, all of us sitting round in their playroom. It used to be Rem and his brother's playroom when they were kids and they'd kind of turned it into a chill room, with a sofa, a massive telly

101

and their Xbox and a big beanbag chair. Aish was in the beanbag, her legs up against the wall, and I was sitting on the floor next to her. The boys were sat on the sofa. Remy and me were drinking a bottle of rum, and the twins just had Coke, although obviously I was spiking Aisha's every time Ash's back was turned. We were watching telly and just chatting, and it felt good, it felt like old times. I don't mean to sound harsh to Eli and Elise, obviously, but it was always the four of us before; it was us four since we were kids.

So yeah, we're hanging at Remy's house, having a few drinks, and even Ash is being fun, he's being like proper, sarcastic Ash, taking the piss out of all of us like he used to. My sides actually hurt by the time Remy said the taxi was there to take us to the party.

It was one of the big houses on the edge of town, one of the new ones in those cul-de-sacs, you know the ones? Hers was a massive one, all white like a wedding cake. Her parents were away for the whole weekend, and the neighbours were some cool young gay couple who didn't care about the noise, so everyone was out in the back garden.

To be honest, all the kids from Remy's gym were dicks. The guys took themselves too seriously and the girls were all really uptight, until they had a drink and then they were a mess. Most of them went to St Agnes's, the fancy school the other side of Kings Lyme, but a couple of them were from our school too. The girl whose party it was was sitting in the middle with a bottle of wine in her hand – she was one of the Aggers bitches and you could tell. She kind of pouted when she saw us and then when Remy walked out behind Aisha, her whole face changed into this super-fake welcoming smile, all 'Hi babe!' and hugs. I swear, she even put a hand on his bicep while she was talking to him. So lame.

Jealous? Nope. Nuh-uh.

Well, to cut the story short, the party was kind of lame too. There was a lot of booze, it had that going for it, and, to be fair, a lot of the Aggers guys are pretty fit. There was this one guy, a footballer I got talking to, who was *gorgeous*. Deacon, I think. Or Damon. Something like that. *Fit*. Anyway, meanwhile Remy's spending the whole night with a crowd of pissed Aggers girls throwing themselves at him, and Aisha and Ash are having a row; I don't know what about. But I was having an okay time. And obviously Remy was. So when the twins said they were going home, we just kind of let them.

I lost Rem for a bit after that. That Deacon guy had disappeared but I was chatting to some other Aggers kids and they were all right. Kind of funny, actually. We were playing stupid drinking games, like really cheesy stuff like I Have Never, and making our way through all of this bitch's mummy and daddy's cognac as we went.

Anyway, at some point I went for a wee and I found Remy in the hallway waiting too. He was pretty sober, actually, compared to everyone else. And yeah, we decided it was kind of over at the party. So we grabbed a couple of bottles of wine from the kitchen and then we left.

I don't know why we went to Elijah's. We just kind of ended up round there, and when we realised we decided to go see him. I don't know, say hi or whatever.

His mum wasn't in, she was probably out in town. Shagging some guy down an alley or in a pub toilet, that's what the rumours were. But – small town. Things get exaggerated. She was probably just having a pint or three. Couldn't fucking blame her.

Anyway, so we knocked but nobody answered. All the lights were on, so we knew Eli was there. We just thought he had his headphones in or something, same as normal, so we let ourselves into the back garden. His room was round the back. We figured we'd just knock on the window, surprise him.

Yeah, we were pretty drunk by then.

Remy saw it first. Them, I mean.

Well, look, you already know, don't you?

Elijah and Elise. Together.

Shagging, all right? They were shagging.

SHE STUMBLES AGAINST the wall as she walks, drunker than she thought when she was sitting. In the hallway, she catches a glimpse of her face: eyes wild, lips dark. The music from downstairs throbs through the floorboards, the sound of laughter drifting up through the open windows.

And then she rounds the corner and sees him standing there.

''Ello 'ello,' he says, the standard Remy greeting, his arms folded, his smile dimpling. 'Having a good time?'

'It's all right. How about you? Mr Unpopular.'

He laughs. 'They just want me for my body.'

She leans against the wall beside him, laughs too. 'Riiight.'

'Seriously though.' He slides a shoulder closer, dips a little to bring his mouth beside her ear. 'What a bunch of dickheads.'

Slowly – or at least it *feels* slow – she turns her head to him. There is an inch between them; it crackles with electricity and then crumples. Her mouth meets his, or his meets hers, she isn't sure – but suddenly they are kissing, hard and fast and dizzying, so that she has to put a hand out to the wall to steady herself.

Remy puts his hands on her shoulders – gently – and pulls back enough to look at her.

'What we doing?' he asks, but before she can answer they are kissing again.

At some point, the person occupying the toilet leaves. At some point, they stagger inside and bolt the door. The tiles are cool against her back but everything else is heat. The music throbs through them and the laughter carries on upwards on the hot night air.

After a while, he pulls away and they laugh, out of breath. His hand is on her thigh and her heart is thumping in her chest. Their eyes meet and he smiles.

'That was . . . different,' he says, and his hand leaves her thigh and pushes his hair away from his face.

She slides down off the sink; shifts away from him, pretending to check her make-up in the mirror. 'Yeah. Crazy night.'

'Gem.' His hand on the small of her back. 'I've been thinking about that happening for ages.'

She turns to look at him. 'Really?'

'Yeah. Course.'

She tries and fails to stop the smile twitching at the corners of her mouth. 'Oh. Cool.'

The hand on her back drops away, grabs hers instead. 'C'mon,' he says. 'Let's get out of here.'

They walk aimlessly at first, wine bottles swinging in their hands. They talk a little, laughing about the people at the party. They don't mention the things that happened in the bathroom, but they're both remembering, both playing it back. For days, she'll remember it in vivid flashes, her skin hot again as she remembers how his hands felt against it. But now they keep talking, they keep laughing, they keep things normal. The road back into town slopes downwards, and they pause at the top, looking out across the fairylit streets, the fields beyond. 'Big world out there,' Remy says, grinning at her, and she remembers, again, that soon this will all be over.

When the road levels out, they wander past darkened houses, their voices dropping to whispers. She remembers his mouth beside her ear in the hallway, goosebumps breaking out across her arms. She drinks more wine, checks her phone. Nothing from Aisha, which surprises her, but she puts the phone away and looks up at the stars.

'Hey,' Remy says. 'Isn't Elijah's house around here somewhere?'

She shrugs. 'Think so.'

'Let's go see him,' he says, setting off. 'Bet he has weed.'

They almost miss the house the first time. A small bungalow in a street of small bungalows, they stand outside and look at the darkened windows.

'You think his mum's in?' Remy asks, looking at the empty drive.

'She's never in,' Gemma replies, taking another swig of wine and moving a little closer. 'But it doesn't look like he is either.'

'He's probably watching porn,' Remy says, and then, for reasons he won't be able to recall later, he sets off across the grass. Gemma follows him, laughing, and they make their way down the dark passage at the side of the house, and through the unlocked garden gate. They stumble against the bricks and laugh, his hand finding her hip in the darkness. She breathes in the smell of him: wine and soap and limes, before he pulls away and rounds the corner of the house.

It's difficult to think of later, difficult to remember it clearly, but Gemma will always be sure, afterwards, that she knew then. Knew that something was wrong, that things were about to change.

She was pretty drunk though.

But she does remember peeping round the corner, watching Remy crawl to the window, peering up over the sill. She remembers seeing his eyes turn wide, remembers his hissed 'You have to see this.'

And she remembers joining him there, remembers looking through the glass, her fingers gripping the sill.

And, of course, she remembers them.

The room is dark, just a flicker of light from the laptop screen where a film is playing out unwatched. The patterned duvet is on the floor; the sheets on the bed, greyish and stained, are tangled around a foot. Two feet. Two mismatched feet, which flex and strain against the fabric.

It takes her a second to process, because their faces are the last things she sees. Elijah's lost in a fold of pillow, his fist bunching it up from beneath. Elise's hidden, at first, by that dark fan of hair as she leans over him, her hands pressed either side of his shoulders.

'Oh my God,' Gemma whispers under her breath, and before she knows what she's doing she's fumbling her phone from her handbag. Before she knows what she's doing – although of course she *does* know, she can't deny that to herself even later – she is holding the phone up, camera app open, her hand resting on the sill for balance.

Remy glances down, sees what she is doing.

'No,' he says, and his hand slams down, taking the phone from her.

And then she watches as he switches the mode from photo to video. She watches as he presses 'Record'.

Interview with Gemma Morris, 27th September, 2016

Well, *yeah*, it was unexpected. I mean, I know I'd been joking about them being the Gruesome Twosome and all that, but it actually *was* a joke. I never thought Elise would go for Eli. Elise was *hot*, way out of his league. And he was so . . . I don't know. Not sexual. I couldn't imagine him even *thinking* about sex.

And then it's there, right in front of my face. I couldn't believe it. In his gross little room with its dirty sheets. And it wasn't even like he'd initiated it – from where I was sitting, she looked *way* more into it than him.

Goes to show, doesn't it? You never know.

We didn't watch for long. Well, not really. I mean, it took us a couple of minutes to realise that it was actually for real. And then we realised that we were actually just sitting watching them bang, and that that was a bit weird, so we legged it.

We carried on walking around for a while, laughing about it and drinking our wine. Yeah, Rem was more surprised than me. He kept going on about how fit Elise was and how he didn't see that coming, and then we sat down and watched the video. It already seemed like we'd imagined it, to be honest.

I don't really know when we decided not to tell the others. I think we talked about it that night. Because even though we thought it was funny, both of us knew that Ash wouldn't approve. He hated stuff like that, gossiping or bitching about people behind their backs. He just hated it. He'd call you out if he heard you doing it, and Ash hated confrontation too, so that should show how much it bothered him.

Anyway, I got home that night and slept for like twelve hours and when I woke up, I had a message from Rem being a bit funny about it. He was like 'Oh I think we were a bit out of order, weren't we?' with a smiley face. Then 'Shall we just keep it between us two?' Winking face. That kind of thing.

But yeah, I got it. I agreed. So we didn't tell Aisha and Ash, we didn't let on to Eli and Elise that we knew. We kept it a secret.

Well, no. I didn't delete the video.

As EXAMS DRAW closer, the gaps between people grow larger. Ash and Elise spend their break-times in revision sessions in the library; Elise and Elijah spend their lunchtimes huddled together, talking in low voices, sharing food. Gemma is bored of all of it. She's figured out exactly which subjects she needs to revise and which she'll be able to safely scrape acceptable grades in, and she doesn't understand the big performance the others are putting into it.

But at least she still has Aisha. One particularly sunny afternoon, with none of the muggy clouds that have filled the past few weeks, she persuades her to bunk off fifth-period maths and the two of them sneak out of the school and down the side street which isn't overlooked by any classrooms.

Once they're clear of the school, they start to relax. Aisha takes a bag of Haribo from her satchel and offers it to Gemma (who takes a fried egg, because they're the ones Aisha likes the least). They walk happily down dappled, leafy streets and then out into the sunshine of the park.

'I'm so glad we didn't go,' Aisha says, sending a little thrill of pleasure through Gemma's heart. 'I totally need a break.'

'Yep.' Gemma squeaks open the gate to the children's playground, which is deserted like it always is. There's a newer, nicer one not far up the road, with special spongy flooring and chunky educational puzzles screwed everywhere. This one is a little unloved, with its fading woodchip floor and its rusted swings, slide and lethal spider-web climbing frame, but it's theirs.

'Go on, give us another egg,' Gemma says, sinking onto one of the swings and letting her bag flop onto the woodchip.

Aisha hands her the packet and starts swinging on the other swing, little-girl style with her legs stretched out and her head tilted back so that her hair streams out behind her. 'I saw Tom the other day,' she says.

'Oh yeah?' Gemma starts swinging too, gently, keeping the tips of her toes on the floor. 'Where?'

'He was parked outside the QuikStop while I was walking home. I saw him getting in his car.'

'Did you say hi?'

Aisha glances sideways, her smooth cheeks kinked in a smile. 'Nope. I crossed the road and kept walking.'

'Good girl.'

'Do you have plans with Paul at the weekend?' Aisha leans further back, almost horizontal on her swing now with her toes pointed like a ballerina's. 'Oh my God, the breeze feels *so* good right now.'

'No.' Gemma gives up on swinging and plucks the Haribo pack from between her thighs. 'I haven't heard from him.'

'Oh.' Aisha stops swinging too, the momentum carrying her back – forth – back – forth before she can drag her feet against the ground to slow herself. 'He's probably just busy?'

Gemma shrugs, careful to keep her *Whatever* face on. 'Probably.' She hands the sweets back to Aisha. 'What you doing?'

Aisha pulls a face. 'We have an auntie's birthday. It's going to be totally boring.'

'Oh boo. Does that mean you can't come out and play?'

'Nah, we'll be home by like seven. Want to do something Saturday night?'

'Yes! We could go into town. We'll totally get in anywhere now. All of the bouncers have seen us with Paul and everyone, they must just think we're at college too.'

Aisha grins. 'You think so?'

'Totally.'

'We could do that.' Aisha folds her legs up so that she's cross-legged, the movement sending the swing creaking back and forth again. Her fingers loop through the chains. 'Or, why don't we have a girly night? Watch movies, eat popcorn, steal all of the duvets? I could *totally* get Mum to bake brownies.'

'No, no, get her to make that opium rice pudding thing again!' Gemma tilts her face back to catch the sun. 'That was *too* delicious.'

Aisha laughs. 'You mean *gasagase payasa*. It has poppy seeds in it, not opium. And it just put you to sleep!'

'Well, that's why they call it a sleepover.' Gemma flops a hand in Aisha's direction and is rewarded with a cola bottle. 'Yeah,' she says, flicking it into her mouth. 'That sounds fun. Let's do that. At yours?' She thinks about this for a second. 'Or I could probably persuade my dad. That way we could sneak booze in.'

Aisha bites her bottom lip, a thing she does when she's about to say something she's not so sure about. 'Or . . . We could ask Elise? Her dad's probably away? We haven't had a sleepover round there in ages?' All of the sentences come out as questions; something else that happens when she isn't so sure about what she's saying.

'That's true.' Gemma leans back, testing the chains with her weight. She lets herself swing a little, pretending to consider this option. 'Do you think Elise would be up for it though? She seems pretty busy with Elijah at the moment.'

'Oh, I think she'd probably like a girly night.' Aisha smooths her hair over one shoulder and starts plaiting it. 'I don't think Elijah can be that much fun to be around.' She hesitates, abandoning her plait and unfolding her legs so that she can swing again. 'I mean, all they're doing is studying, right? We need to get them out, having some fun.'

But Gemma isn't fooled. 'Why don't you think Eli's fun to be around? What's happened?'

Aisha makes a surprised face, and not a very good one. 'Nothing's happened! I just don't know if it's that great that they're hanging out all the time.'

Gemma knows better than to keep asking questions; she just carries on watching her friend. Not staring, just watching. The same way Elijah does, she thinks suddenly, and feels bad. Aisha pushes herself forward on the swing a little more forcefully a couple of times and then gives up. 'Okay, look, fine. I found out something about Eli. I'm worried about it. I'm worried that *he's* worried about it.'

Gemma pulls herself upright on the swing. 'What?'

'It's just . . . You know how Derran said that thing to him in biology, about his sister? And then he went crazy and attacked him?'

115

Gemma doesn't really need to nod – of *course* she remembers – but she does.

'Well, after that, I did a bit of, I don't know, research, and I found out a lot about his sister.'

'*What* about her?'

'Umm. She had, like, a kind of breakdown at their old school. Like saying that everyone was evil and she wanted to kill them all. She was taking something. It got pretty . . . it was really bad. It was in the papers a lot.'

Gemma jolts up in her swing, the chains jangling. 'What the . . . ?'

'Yeah, I know. It's horrible, right? Imagine what that must've been like for him.'

'Shit. That's twisted.'

'I know.'

'Why didn't he tell us?'

Aisha looks down, her shadow jagged over the shards of wood. 'Maybe he just wanted a fresh start.'

Gemma feels a guilty pang at that. 'Yeah, I guess. Man. Do the others know?'

'Ash does, I think. I haven't asked him. I don't think Rem does.'

'Derran will tell everyone.'

Aisha glances hopefully at her. 'He hasn't so far. I don't think he actually knows anything.'

'You think he just got lucky and hit a nerve?'

'Yeah.'

Gemma thinks about this, idly swinging a couple of times. 'Well, maybe. I hope so. Cos if that gets round, think about what he'd do. If that's what he did to Derran for even mentioning her.'

'I know.'

'But I see what you mean about Elise.' Gemma has fumbled her phone from her bag, is busy searching. 'It's Rian, right? His sister's name? Oh my God, this is nuts.' She watches the clip that Aisha had to turn off and her face pales. 'Wow. Do you think Elise knows?'

Aisha is chewing her lip again. 'I don't know. But we can't say anything, Gem. It's Eli's secret to tell, not ours. And it's not like *he* did it, is it?'

Gemma pauses, thumb hovering over the 'Replay' icon. 'Well, yeah. I guess not. It's still pretty messed-up though.'

'Yeah, for *him*.' Aisha's eyes are wide; Gemma worries she can see the beginning of tears there.

'Yeah, that sucks,' she says, feeling bad. 'God, poor Eli. No wonder he's glued to a screen the whole time. He's probably waiting for news on her, right?'

Aisha shrugs. 'Maybe. You won't say anything, will you?'

'Course not.'

'So . . . Should we ask Elise to come this weekend?'

'Yeah—' Gemma starts. 'Oh, wait, she said she was going away, didn't she? Some trip with her dad? London or something?'

'Oh yeah.' Aisha sinks back in her swing, deflated. 'That's good for her, I guess. When was the last time she even mentioned him? At least he's taking an interest now.'

'Well, we can invite her out next weekend, once she's back.'

'Yeah, good plan.'

'But should we do something about Eli now? Should we have a word with Derran and tell him to keep it to himself?'

Aisha thinks about this for a while. 'No, I don't think we should get involved. If Derran was going to say something, I think he would've by now? So maybe he doesn't know anything?' She looks down, scuffing the woodchip with the toe of a shoe. 'No, I think we should just stay out of it. I mean, Eli seems to be doing okay, right? He seems to be dealing with it his own way.'

*Conversation from online gaming forum, 5-star,
7th May, 2015*

truthteller
anyone ever think there just isn't actually a point
to anything?

betaboy
lol whats up dude

hunter_s
aww sounds like bella trouble

truthteller
not everything is about girls

truthteller
some things are more important

the_jump
dude what happened?

truthteller
why do the people you love always do the most
fucked-up things?

truthteller
you can't trust anyone. can't rely on anyone

betaboy
people are messed up man. it sucks

the_jump
sorry mate

the_jump
you got us tho. lol

bangsaidthegun
^^^what he said

bangsaidthegun
we here for you bro

truthteller
thanks

truthteller
good to know people out there who get how fucked
everything is

bangsaidthegun
oh we know bro

bangsaidthegun
this is the only real place there is

truthteller
@bangsaidthegun I think you might actually be
right there

Interview with Aisha Kapoor, 28th September, 2016

I did tell Gem about Rian in the end – I didn't really mean to, it just kind of came out. But I'd been *so* worried about it, you know, and I guess it was good to share the secret, to kind of see what she thought. And also I could tell that she was getting fed up of Eli and Elise going off just the two of them, so I wanted her to understand why Eli was the way he was, if that makes sense?

Things had started feeling really weird that last couple of weeks. There was all this unspoken stuff – things that I was keeping secret from Ash, and things Elijah was keeping secret from us, except that we knew the secret and the fact that we *knew* was a secret too. It all felt horrible and tangled up and like we just weren't close any more. I even got a weird feeling around Remy and Gemma when they were together, like they had something they weren't telling us. I always wondered if something happened

122

after Ash and me left that party at Remy's friend's house.

So I was feeling a bit sad about it all, and still feeling worried about school and exams and whatever came after, which still just felt like a massive question mark, if you know what I mean? This big blank space where I was supposed to have a plan.

Oh. Umm. Yeah. It was a Monday, I think, but it was after school. I didn't actually know anything about it till I got home from school. It was actually Ash who told me.

The Head called Ash in after fourth period and told him – I think Miss Wu had told her that he and Eli were close. They knew it was going to be in all the papers so I guess they wanted someone to be there once it got round school. I guess they wanted Ash to tell all of us too, so we could be ready. So we could be there for Eli, you know?

So yeah. I got home that afternoon and Ash and my mum were sitting at the kitchen table, and Ash was *crying*. Well, not actually crying, but kind of wet-eyed and shaky, you know. My mum had made chai, proper masala chai, with a strainer and everything, so I knew it was serious.

It was weird, I felt like I was, I don't know, intruding when I put my bag down and sat with them. Like, Mum poured me a cup but neither of them said anything. Ash just kept looking at me but it was like he couldn't really get the words out. And

Mum was kind of waiting for him to, like stroking his hand and saying 'It's okay, *Beta*, it will be okay.' So, you know, I asked what was going on.

And they told me.

WhatsApp conversation between Aisha Kapoor, Gemma Morris and Remy Dixon, 7th May, 2015

Aisha: Gem, u heard what's happened?
Gem: no what?
Aisha: eli
Aisha: his sister died
Gemma: wtf
Gemma: seriously???
Aisha: yeah. not sure on details but it sounds like it might've been on purpose
Aisha: it's horrible
Gemma: fucking hell
Gemma: hold on, adding Rem
Gemma: rem, eli's sister died
Remy: whaaaat the fuck
Remy: shit
Remy: that's awful
Aisha: yeah
Aisha: what do we do?
Aisha: should we go over there?

Aisha: Ash says no but i feel like we should
Remy: nah i think Ash is right
Remy: let him tell us in his own time
Remy: he's a pretty private guy
Gemma: Aish, u spoken to Elise?
Aisha: no
Aisha: she's not answering her phone
Aisha: she never does, so annoying
Gemma: k
Remy: u think he'll come to school tomo?
Remy: what's Ash gonna do?
Aisha: Ash is trying to call him but he won't pick up
Aisha: the house phone doesn't even ring
Remy: what's his mum gonna do, she's already a nightmare
Remy: poor kid
Gemma: so sad
Aisha: yeah
Aisha: hold on, i think Ash is talking to him
Gemma: k babe

[there is a break in the conversation of 11 minutes]

Aisha: ok
Aisha: he's all right
Aisha: Ash just talked to him, he said he sounds ok
Aisha: sad obviously
Aisha: but he doesn't want any fuss, he doesn't want anyone to know

Aisha: so you guys need to pretend u don't know, k?

Aisha: he'll prob tell u eventually but just in case

Remy: yeah sure

Remy: glad ash got thru to him

Remy: so fucked up

Gemma: my lips are sealed babe

Gemma: is he coming in tomo?

Aisha: no

Aisha: he's gonna look after his mum

Remy: ahh mate

Remy: imagine

Aisha: g2g

Aisha: want to check on Ash

Aisha: see u guys tomorrow

Gemma: see u tomorrow babe xxx

Remy: c u tomo Aish

Remy: give Ash a hug from me x

THERE IS NO Elijah the next day or the next one after that. They meet at the school gates before registration, something they haven't done since the beginning of Year 10, when they were new, when they were just starting out as a group. Ash and Aisha arrive first, huddling together under the sparse shade of a blossom tree. The sun is already high in the sky and the air is thick and difficult to breathe.

Gemma arrives next, school shirt unbuttoned to reveal a crop top, her face half-hidden by Hollywood-star sunglasses.

'This has got to be the first time I've ever been fifteen minutes early for school,' she says, tipping her chin down so that the glasses slide down the bridge of her nose. 'You proud of me, Ash?'

Ash laughs. 'Definitely.'

Remy turns up then, aviators pushed up on his head, a can of Red Bull in hand. 'Oi oi,' he says, ruffling Ash's hair and holding out a fist for Aisha to bump. 'Been a while since we did this.'

And then, finally, five minutes before the bell, Elise. Aisha can't help noticing how dirty her hair is, how her usually perfect eyeliner looks dried and smudged, like she slept in

128

yesterday's. *But that's normal*, she reminds herself. *A really bad thing just happened to our friend; who cares about eyeliner now?* She holds an arm out to hug Elise and is sad by how stiff her friend feels as she does, at how weird it is for them to even touch each other.

'You speak to Eli last night?' Remy asks Ash.

Ash nods, glancing at Elise. 'He's okay. Well, obviously not okay. But he's doing all right.'

'Well, good,' Gemma says, pushing her glasses back up her nose. 'But what we gonna do about this place? People are gonna find out. It's already in the papers, I checked.'

Remy scoffs. 'What we meant to do? We can't stop people talking.'

'Yeah, but we could set the story straight,' Aisha says. 'Make sure people aren't saying horrible stuff about her. Or about Eli. I really don't want him to come back to loads of mean rumours.'

Ash is frowning, a hand pressed to his mouth the way he does when he's thinking. 'Okay,' he says eventually. 'How about, if we hear anyone talking about it today, we tell them the whole story. We make sure they know that she was ill, that it's really sad and not okay to laugh about. But we don't bring it up otherwise. I don't know how many people would know she was Elijah's sister. It didn't say it in the news story you read, right?'

Gemma shakes her head. 'Nope. It said she had a brother but it didn't name him.'

'Okay, so probably no one's gonna know,' Remy says. 'I think Ash is right. Let's not jump in and make it everyone's business if we don't have to.'

Aisha notices the way Gemma shoots him a secret sideways smile; just for a second. She doesn't like it.

'Okay, good,' Ash says. 'And I'll go and see Elijah tonight. I'll let you guys know how he's doing.'

This time Aisha looks at Elise. Her face is pale and sickly, her eyes darting back and forth across the people coming in through the gate. 'We can't let them talk about him,' she says, her voice hoarse. 'He won't be able to take it.'

'We won't,' Aisha says, slipping an arm around her again. This time, Elise relaxes into it. 'We'll protect him.'

'Course we will.' Remy punches Elise's shoulder, one of his highest displays of affection. 'Come on, let's go in. Together.'

Elise nods, and the five of them walk out into the sunshine, across the playground towards the dark mouth of the mirrored doors to the school reception. It feels good; it feels powerful. They are a group again. They will protect Elijah. Aisha feels as if a terrible weight which has been pressing down on her since last night has suddenly been lifted, just a little.

It's only as they pass through the doors into the air-conditioned reception that Elise's nails dig into her arm. Aisha turns, the others carrying on ahead of them, the second set of double doors which lead through to the science block and their form rooms squeaking shut behind them. It's just Aisha and Elise, alone in the cool, dim foyer, even the receptionist away from his desk.

'We can't let them talk about him,' Elise whispers, her eyes searching Aisha's face (Aisha swears she can *feel* it, a crawling sensation over her skin). 'He won't like it. He won't be able to stand it.'

Aisha nods, her eyes travelling down to the place where Elise's fingertips are still digging into her arm. 'I know. It's okay.'

But Elise is shaking her head.

'It's *not* okay,' she says. 'He won't be able to take it.'

Interview with Gemma Morris, 27th September, 2015

I think it was three days Elijah was off in the end. It definitely wasn't a whole week. But yeah, by the time he got back, everyone knew. It was in all the papers. I remember seeing it on the MailOnline when I was looking at the celebrity gossip at lunchtime. I can't remember the headline they used. Something about a 'Psycho Schoolgirl'. I couldn't click on it. Think of the comments. But I read the stuff on the BBC about it. They had pictures of her diaries and stuff, all the things she wrote. It was awful. She was properly ill. Nobody seemed to get that.

Of course we did, babe. We had a deal, the five of us. If we heard someone talking about it, we called them out. We told them the truth. None of this 'Psycho Schoolgirl' bullshit. None of this devil-worshipping family crap. We set it out straight. Eli's sister fell into a bad crowd, she took a load of mind-bending drugs, she had a breakdown. We made them feel *bad*. We made them see how sad it was. And yeah, after a day or so, people left it alone. They were probably all still gossiping about it, obviously, but at least it was in secret. We felt pretty sure nobody would say anything to *him* about it.

And when he came back, he never mentioned it. I mean, I probably didn't expect him to right away. Where do you even start explaining how you feel about something like that? And it's not like Eli was the kind of person to sit around talking about feelings in the first place. I kind of assumed he was talking to Ash about it, and Elise obviously. The rest of us, we just sort of told him how sorry we were and he just kind of nodded and looked away and that was pretty much it. That feels pretty shitty now but what were we supposed to do? *Force* him to talk about it?

Yeah, the blog was still there, although obviously people weren't talking about it as much with all that going on. I think it got updated a couple of days after we heard about Eli's sister. That was the first post. But it was just some random gossip about some bitchy girl in the popular crowd. It was kind of funny – something about her blowing some other chick's dad for acne drugs? I don't know. I don't even know if it was true, although the guy in question was a doctor and she did have really clear skin, the girl. But we weren't really in the mood for funny.

A couple of days later, there was some post about one of the kids on the football team shagging a teacher. But there's always rumours like that. No one really believed it. Although now, I wonder. Everything else turned out to be true.

Then there was one about the girl in our year who was bulimic, like that's something to gossip about. That was the day after, I think. It started getting much faster then: stuff every day, everyone wondering who was going to be next.

And yeah, then it happened. A couple of days later, a week before exams started.

That post.

That fucking post.

GEMMA IS THE first one to see it. She jerks awake at 5 a.m. after a bad dream, the air in her room so hot and thick it feels like it's pressing down on her. She pushes the window open and lies back down. The neighbourhood outside is silent and still, but it's *too* quiet, she can *hear* the silence. She flicks through her phone for a while, one eye closed. When she's sure she won't be going back to sleep, she sits up and rotates through the same old circuit again: Instagram, Facebook, Twitter. Refresh Twitter, refresh Twitter, check Instagram again.

After a while, she gets bored. She flicks through tabloid sites, reading articles about celebrity babies and celebrity break-ups. The thought of gossip makes her think of the blog, and after she's bored of reading about a movie star cheating on another movie star, she types in the address. She wants to see the comments people have left on the post about the girl in their year with bulimia. She wants to know if people are as angry about it as she is.

But now there's a new post at the top of the page. She flops onto her back, the phone held up over her face, and scrolls down.

And then she sits up. Reads it again.

Guess which Year 11 good Hindu girl just had to get an abortion? That'll teach you to sleep with a college kid who gives exactly zero fucks.

Wonder what Mummy and Daddy will say?

Her heart has started pounding so hard she thinks she can actually hear it. She flicks back up and reads the sentences again, trying to analyse, trying to quell the panic. She hasn't told anyone; has she?

No. She hasn't; she knows she hasn't. And Aisha wouldn't either. Panic becomes anger, and she throws back her covers and swivels to sit on the edge of the bed, still staring at the screen. Clearly, Tom has told someone. Someone who has told someone else who has told some other people who have told some other people, until the person who is behind this blog hears it too. Hears it and posts it here, for everyone to see.

She thinks about it for a while, wondering who she should tell. Eventually, she has to admit it: there's only one person she trusts with this.

Waking up, Remy performs his usual routine too. He rolls onto his front, grunts, and pushes his face deeper into the pillow, his hand fumbling for the alarm and the snooze button. After it's gone off another two times, he finally pushes himself onto his forearms. He reaches out for his phone, the other hand scrubbing sleep from his eyes, and he unlocks it to see five WhatsApp messages from Gemma. He reads through them, his sleepy expression slowly tightening into a frown, and then he rolls onto his back and reads them again.

At school, she's waiting for him on the front steps as he locks his bike into the rack.

'Did you read it?'

'Yeah.' He chews his lip. 'Is it true? About Aish?'

'Yes.' No point in hiding it now, she reasons. 'She's gonna lose it when she sees.'

'Well, it doesn't mention her by name,' Remy reasons.

Gemma glares at him. 'It doesn't have to. Hello? That's the trouble with going to a stupid white-washed school in the suburbs. Aisha's like, the only Hindu girl in Year 11.'

'There's Saanvi Subramanium.'

She rolls her eyes. 'Yeah. Like anyone's gonna think it's her.'

'Okay. So what do we do?'

She shakes her head, looks back at the canteen window. 'We need to get them to take it down. I'm going to talk to that twat Tom. Find out who he told. Hopefully that'll help us figure out who's writing the blog.'

Remy frowns. 'How can you be so sure it was him? He's not exactly gonna be broadcasting it, is he?'

Gemma looks at him, impatient.

'Is there definitely no one else that Aisha told?' he prompts.

She's about to turn away when suddenly it strikes her. Her eyes narrow.

'That bitch,' she says.

Once I started thinking about it, it all started to fall into place. When you looked at the blog, almost everyone who'd had a story about them on there were people who'd picked on Elijah in the past. It was totally him. I felt stupid I hadn't even thought of it before.

And I knew Aisha had told Elise about the abortion. So Elise had *obviously* told Elijah when they were all cosied up in his skanky bedroom.

The thing I didn't get was *why*. Why he'd post it up like that. What had Aisha done to him? She was always a sweetheart to everyone. She was off sick that day so I kept hoping she wouldn't have seen it, hoping I could get it sorted before she even had to know. But then more and more people started talking about it – I could hear them whispering when I walked past on the way to lessons, when me and Rem bunked off at lunchtime. I hated that, all of them gossiping about her. It wasn't *fair*.

And Remy just didn't get it. 'It's nothing to be ashamed of,' he kept saying. 'If anyone should be embarrassed it's that Tom prick. Not Aish.'

But it was *private*, that's the thing. It was Aisha's business, nobody else's. And Elijah would've have known how crazy her parents would go about something like that. How crazy even Ash would go. So why did it end up there anyway? What did she do wrong?

Remy kept trying to think of other people it could be. I guess he just didn't want to think that our friends would do that. But once I knew, I just *knew*. I kept picturing Eli hunched over his phone at lunch, him and Elise whispering to each other.

Yeah, I probably *would've* just gone right over and asked them. But Remy told me not to. I guess he didn't want me to cause a big fight over nothing if I was wrong, so he said that we had to find out, to be sure.

So yeah.

We went back to Eli's that night.

IT'S ALREADY TOO late of course. Aisha saw the post only a couple of hours after Gemma did, and so she didn't show up to school. She's lying at home, in bed, with the curtains drawn, pretending to have a stomach bug. It's not hard; she can't move without feeling sick. Her parents have gone to work, leaving tea and sympathy and kisses to the forehead. These things only make her feel sicker.

She's wondering how long it will be before Ash sees the post; before Ash hears the story second-, third-, fourth-, tenth-hand from someone in the corridor or in the canteen. Ash is perhaps the only person who might believe, just for a second, that it's Saanvi Subramanium, a truly good Hindu girl, that the post is referring to. This will seem the more likely conclusion, as far as he is concerned. He might have warned her, those weeks ago, to be careful, but to Ash that means not walking home alone at night; not neglecting school work in favour of fun; not hanging out in places where people might get 'the wrong idea' about her. It would never cross his mind (at least, Aisha doesn't think it would) that, in fact, it might be the right idea entirely.

But Aisha knows that won't last long. Whispers will start, and then louder ones. People who've seen Aisha in town; people who've seen Aisha drunk at parties. The whole truth of it will slowly unravel and her calm, logical twin will have to accept it. His sister is a stranger.

She thinks back to a time when they were little, maybe six or seven. Their birthday, all of the family crowded round, watching them as they open their presents. A cake on the table; three layers, lemon buttercream icing and their names swirled across the top. When the presents are open and the family has dispersed – the women in the kitchen, drinking tea and watching her dad and uncle prepare the lunch, the other men lingering in the doorway and the garden – she stands alone and looks up at it. The icing so thick she can still see the marks from the palette knife, the lemon smell making her mouth water. She doesn't even think about it; she reaches out and runs a finger around the edge. It curls in her mouth like lemon peel and the sweetness explodes inside her. She examines the cake but she has been careful, there's barely a mark. As the mouthful dissolves, she takes another. And another and another, taking less care as the sugar buzzes through her. And then the sound of an auntie outside, on her way back from the bathroom, and she flees, frightened, to find Ash and her cousins in the garden, her teeth on edge with sweetness.

After lunch, when it's time for cake, her crime is discovered. Her mother stands in front of the cake, as if she's too ashamed for anyone to see it with those gaps, those places where the sponge is exposed. 'Who did this?' she says, and her eyes settle on Aisha. '*Beta*, you were here alone. Did you eat some?'

She would have confessed, she knows she would. But of course Ash steps forward, his hands behind his back, his face entirely serious. 'No, Mummyji. Aisha wouldn't do such a thing.'

And because he says it, they believe it. *Aisha wouldn't do such a thing.* The cake is cut, the gaps forgotten. In private, her parents blame one of her uncles, drunk as usual.

Guess which Year 11 good Hindu girl just had to get an abortion?

Wonder what Mummy and Daddy will say?

She flops onto her back and tries to sleep. Tries to get rid of the sour taste, almost like lemon, which keeps rising in her mouth.

She refuses dinner, pretends to sleep when Ash pokes his head round her door. He retreats quickly and that makes her think that perhaps he hasn't heard yet. This is almost worse; it means more waiting, the whole truth of it hovering over her like a cartoon anvil, ready to come crashing down. It could be tomorrow, someone shouting it across the playground, or it could be tonight, when he finally quits revision for the night and logs idly into his little-used Facebook. Later, much later, when they've all gone to bed and the house is quiet again, Aisha dares to check hers. Thirty-five new messages in her inbox; her cursor hovers over the icon but she can't quite bring herself to click. She steels herself to look at the newsfeed instead, her confidence growing as she scans through the first updates. People are talking about their dinner, their evenings, the latest stupid reality show. They are posting pictures, funny quotes. She starts to relax; maybe people don't care about the blog after all.

And then there's the first one. Some girl from her year, a name she barely recognises. *lol got to love a secret slag,* it says. *it's always the quiet ones right!*

Underneath it, people have commented. *Haha totally is!* writes a guy from Aisha's geography class. *Guess they don't have condoms where she comes from*, another, unknown name writes, and her mouth fills with a sicky, stale taste.

There's another status an hour earlier, this one including the link to the blog itself. A boy from her maths class, Sean, who posts a wide-eyed, blushing emoji. *Oh dear . . . didn't know she had it in her!*

Lol, someone else comments. *Sounds like she's had a lot in her!*

stupid bitch. Some guy she's never heard of before.

She rolls onto her side, lets the phone drop back down to the bed. She's surprised to find she can't cry. She feels numb, nothing but numbness. The clock clicks past midnight, and the only sound is the soft snoring from her parents' room.

After a while, she picks up the phone again, refreshes her feed. Her eyes narrow; at first she thinks it hasn't loaded properly, because every post she sees is the same. The same video posted again and again as she watches, people sharing it with 'LOL's and shocked smileys. *Whoaaaa*, Sean writes when he shares it. *Go on lad!*

And this is when Aisha feels the first pang of dread. She feels like throwing the phone across the room, but instead she clicks 'Play' on the video. She watches it.

A darkened room. The flickering light from a laptop. Legs intertwined, a fan of dark hair falling forward.

'Oh my God,' she whispers.

truthteller
u guys. help pls. cant take it any more. i want to pulp their tiny brains out.

Dx99
dude. we here for you. dont let the bellas get you down.

betarevolution
^^^ what he said

truthteller
thanks man. im just so sick of their bullshit. its like poison everywhere, like a beehive of toxic shit

bangsaidthegun
been there man. fear not. the betas will have their time.

nuguy
hey truthteller. where u go to school?

truthteller
@nuguy south east of england man. edward n bella capital of the uk.

truthteller
@bangsaidthegun yeah dude. and im thinking that time is now.

bangsaidthegun
lol what u got planned soldier?

truthteller
like ur username says man. bang bang bye bye

betarevolution
yeah man! DO IT

thejump
u serious @truthteller? that shit needs some planning

truthteller
im serious guys. i got what i need. and they're gonna get what they deserve

betarevolution
shit yeah! whens this going down @truthteller?

truthteller

@betarevolution tomorrow brother. any of you guys go to school round my parts, time to skip it

betarevolution

yes brother! i got goosebumps right now

thejump

@truthteller u for real? u thought this out? where u get a gun in d uk? whats the security like in ur school?

truthteller

@thejump its sorted mate. security no problem

halo_guy

DUDES. wtf. don't even joke about this stuff

Dx99

@halo_guy fuck off man. @truthteller is bringing our message to UK shores. there are plenty of gaming forums out there for you, leave us to bring the change

halo_guy

bring what change? ur a bunch of lil boys who cant get laid, grow up and stop talking this sick crap before MI5 pick u up

betarevolution

@halo_guy go play somewhere else. u no idea what u talking about

@truthteller dude. this is your special night. tomorrow u make the world a better place. u make urself a name.

hugo_first

lols imagine if this was true

bangsaidthegun

i believe him. truthteller don't lie to us

killerkenny

if he serious he needs to get them in one room. Say they hostages then kill them all. and lock the doors from the inside. chains if you can. slow the police down.

betarevolution

^^ this aint bad advice @truthteller

halo_guy

seriously, wtf is wrong with you guys? what, you get rejected a coupla times and now you want to kill ur whole school. That's messed up.

truthteller
@halo_guy they're the ones who are messed up. And tomorrow they're going to pay.

Interview with Gemma Morris, 27th September 2016

Look, what can I say? We saw them. We went over there, me and Rem, and we snuck into his garden again. And there they were, just like I knew they would be. The two of them in Eli's bedroom, looking at his laptop and laughing. Writing a new post.

We *saw* them. The blog was right there. They were typing. They were *laughing*.

So yeah. I lost my temper, okay? Wouldn't you? If it was your friend?

You know what I did. You already know.

I don't *want* to say it. You *already know*.

Okay, fine. I took my phone and I hit upload. If they were going to do that to my friend, I was gonna show them how it felt. It was *their* turn to have their secrets out there for everyone to see.

I didn't know, did I?

I didn't know what would happen.

Interview with Remy Dixon, 28th September, 2016

Look, I ain't sayin anything about Gem. I know people keep trying to put the blame on her, but that's twisted, man. That's not right. We couldn't have known what was going on. It's *not* Gem's fault. And they never traced that video back to her anyway.

Oh, right. Did she? Well, fair enough. It's her story to tell I guess.

Look, my side of it is: I liked them both. Elise and Elijah were quiet and I never spent much time with them but I never thought they'd do something as fucked up as that. When Gem came to me and said she thought it was Elijah who was posting that blog stuff, I thought she had it totally wrong. But she was pretty convinced, going on about Elise and some night out they'd had, and so I kind of went along with it, thinking there was no chance she'd find anything.

And then we show up at Eli's house, and it's all dark again. Well, I guess we know now that it was always like that, huh? His mum always out doing her thing. Can't really blame her, can you? After what happened with his sister.

Anyways, we snuck round the side again and this time there was a light on in Eli's room. So we kind of took it in turns to peep round the corner and look through the window. They were both in there, Eli and Elise. Laughing. With the laptop open. It took me a couple of looks but yeah, it was definitely the website. I'm pretty sure.

Pretty sure, yeah. No, it was. It definitely was.

They were typing something new, I dunno what. I can't remember if there was a post after Aish's – that one just sticks out, yeah? Whatever happened after is a bit of a blur. Sure they had plenty stored up though. Elise knew a lot of stuff about Gem, sure she'd've shown up at some point.

The funny thing is, yeah, I remember looking at Gem when it was her turn to watch. You'd think she'd have been raging. You'd think she'd have barged in there and laid into them. She's got a right temper on her, Gem. But she just had this look on her face. Like calm. I guess cos she knew she was right. And she already knew exactly what to do, didn't she?

Nah, I didn't see her post the video. We just sat there in the garden for a bit and watched them. They didn't bang or anything, you wouldn't even think they ever had if you didn't already know. She was sitting on the edge of the bed and he was at his desk, with the laptop kinda halfway between them, I didn't even see them touch. Anyways, then we both went home. By the time I get back to mine and check Facebook, there it is. It already had like 100 shares, right, people commenting on it like crazy. It spread so fast, it was insane.

The problem I have is that I swear I saw them laughing. We both did. But now – fuck. I don't know why I'm saying this, it's twisted. Wow.

Now, when I remember it, they're crying.

I don't even know which is true, sometimes.

THE VIDEO IS all anyone can talk about. Their names echo everywhere; the crackly quiet of the video repeating through the speakers of every phone in school.

Gemma can hear her own breathing; the moments when she leant too close to the phone and the recording picks up her laughter; the single time she said 'Oh my God' again to Remy. She walks past people watching the video in registration, by the lockers, in the playground; she hears herself. She hears herself and she knows what they're all seeing, she knows that they're watching the same scene she saw through that window. Something private that happened between two people she calls (called) friends. She tries not to feel guilty; she tries to remember what they did to Aisha. But it chews at her, it finds its way in. She sees the way the story is spreading, the way that same half-caught laugh of hers is replayed over and over while a hundred pairs of eyes watch Elise's body writhe over Elijah's, and she feels sick.

Aisha watches it unfold online. She sits and refreshes and refreshes and refreshes the page and she watches the number of views jump up and up. The number of shares grows and grows and the comments get more disgusting. They talk about the way Elise's body looks: they say that she is too flabby, they say that she's too skinny. I like a bit of meat, they write. I want something to hold onto. They say that she doesn't know what she's doing, they say she's doing it wrong, they say she loves it. They say, they say, they say. Elise has weird nipples. Elise should be a porn star. Elise can't get enough. Elise needs a good seeing to. Elise is a slag. A virgin. Elise can bounce on mine any time she wants. Elise isn't getting anywhere near mine. Elise is filth; Elise is a legend.

Elijah is a loser.

All Elijah can do is lie there.

He must be drunk, the comments say. He must be gay. He must be the only boy in the world who'd let someone as hot as Elise ride him and not even smile.

What an idiot, they say. They say, they say, they say. What a pathetic limpdick loser. Why doesn't he turn her over and give her what she deserves? Why doesn't he reach up and squeeze those puppies? Why doesn't he slap that slag?

Why doesn't he *do* something?

Extract from the private blog of Ashok 'Ash' Kapoor,
14th May, 2015

I don't understand. I don't think I will ever understand
the secrets people keep, the lives we lead when we
think no one is looking.

E & E. The mess this has made. How could I not see?

The things people write online are more evil than
I could ever imagine. I've been trying not to look at
the link but I can't help myself, I have to know. The
things these people are saying about my friends. My
closest friends in all the world.

How is it possible that the authors of these
comments are the people I spend my days with?
People I say hello to, people I sit beside in class? Such
simple, easy evil. Anonymous, online. Say what you
feel. Nobody can stop you.

But how can nobody see that they are people too?
That they have feelings? That those words typed so
easily onto a screen are at the same time being burned
into someone's heart? How can these people not see

that they are doing damage that can never be erased? The internet moves quickly but the things we post to it are there forever.

This is forever. This will never go away.

It is a beautiful night, the fullest full moon he has ever seen. He walks out into the garden barefoot, feeling the first dew against his skin. He holds his purchase in his left hand, heavy against his side. Not heavy at all, when he thinks about it, though it lags and drags in his grip, as if reluctant to be held.

He walks on and on, down the garden, the damp grass swishing at the cuffs of his jeans. When he gets to the splintered old gate, it's already unbolted, already half-open. The hinges shriek as he pulls it closed behind him. Nobody to hear them. He walks on, out into the alley behind the houses, the road smooth and still almost sun-warmed beneath his feet.

There isn't far to walk. Across a footbridge, under the dry, disapproving shadow of the weeping willow, and into the woods proper. A sparse, scrubby expanse of woods, a small, dirty stream running through it. A place which could once have been beautiful but is now littered with condoms and cigarette packets, bright and broken bottles.

He finds the place and stands to look around. His feet feel sticky with the dew now, a splinter of glass piercing his heel. He has cut his hand without realising, and the blood drips down his fingers and tick-tocks against the grass.

He takes a deep breath; breathes in the muggy green smell of the stream, the last musty traces of the cider bottles and cans of Special Brew. He looks back at the faint lights of the houses through the trees. He thinks of them all, all of their faces, laughing laughing laughing. He thinks of the way his sister used to smile, the way she looked behind finger-smeared glass in her locked-down room in the unit.

He lifts up his hand, looks at the object again. So small, so simple. So solid; the only solid thing he has felt in weeks.

He hitches it up, he loops it around a branch in the tree. He thinks of their faces; he tries not to think. It is quiet and he wants it to be quiet, all of it to be quiet. He makes the knot just the way the video showed him online, tests its strength with his weight.

The box is where he left it: a plastic crate he and Elise brought out here once with bottles inside, just the two of them talking in the quiet green, their laughter soft and secret. He puts it in place now, the first wind in weeks lifting the hair away from his face.

When he kicks it away, he thinks of his sister again.

Soft dark hair, that smile, that smile.

Her chewed-down nails, the finger-smeared glass.

Her eyes meeting his; her fingers beckoning him on.

Interview with Remy Dixon, 28th September, 2016

Where was I when I heard? Can't remember, to be honest. I know I was out. I know I got a call from Aisha. And then I was running. Just like that.

I went round to Aish and Ash's place. She'd asked me to, cos Ash was in a bit of a state. Well, not a state, not really. With Ash it was all inside, yeah? So he was just kinda sitting there, not saying much. Kinda staring at the wall. Aisha was crying her eyes out but that just seemed to make Ash go even quieter. He ain't even really looked at her, or me. I've gone round to help and all I end up doing is sitting there next to him, looking at the same patch of wall, with Aisha crying on my shoulder.

I didn't talk to Gem. I couldn't, to be honest. Didn't know what to say. Obviously Aish was trying to call her, but it just kept going to voicemail.

Nah, I don't think I thought of the video then. Couldn't really connect the two – I know it was kinda bad, it being out there like that, but to kill yourself over it? I guess I didn't think he'd do that, not right

159

away. He had a lot of stuff going on, I dunno. My main priority was Ash. Ash was a mess.

I didn't even think of Elise at first. That's well bad, isn't it? I forgot about her.

And the others didn't mention her either, not for ages. It was only after Ash got up – he just stands up and leaves, right, without saying a word. We just thought he'd gone to the bog till we heard the front door go – yeah, so that was when Aisha and me actually sat and talked about it all properly. She told me how some woman walking her dog had found Eli in those woods behind his house, and she told me that it was Eli's mum who called Ash and told him. That kind of surprised me actually. The impression we always got was that his mum didn't even know he had friends, let alone who any of us were.

That's when Aish asks me if I think it was cos of the video. I just said no, not likely, Eli wouldn't do something like that over something so stupid. I told her that we probably didn't know the half of it, like things were probably really fucked up with him. And that made her cry again – to be honest, that made me cry. He was s'posed to be our friend, and we didn't even know he had all this stuff going on. I wish I'd asked him, helped him – course I did.

So Aish and me had our little cry together and then we broke out a bottle of voddy she had stashed in her wardrobe. And when she goes off to try calling Ash again, and that's when I suddenly thought about her.

That's when I thought about Elise.

Conversation from online gaming forum, 5-star, 15th May, 2015

Dx99
holy fuck u guys watching this?

bangsaidthegun
fuckkkkk he did it!!! @truthteller did it!

notnige
whoa

the day of the betas is here friends!!!

miguelonthemic
incredible scenes boys

bangsaidthegun
shit this is insane

i got goosebumps

hugo_first
mate. i did not see this coming

thejump
HERO

killerkenny
check out his score though. not even in double figures
if news is right

halo_guy
jesus christ. it's not a SCORE, it's people's lives. wtaf
is wrong with you guys. this is horrific.

Dx99
watch out boys, i think halo_guy is going to tell on us

bangsaidthegun
he got a teacher! yes my brother!

thejump
cant wait to see the pics. bet they're all bella bitches.

Dx99
@thejump for sure

bangsaidthegun
oh man this is epic

miguelonthemic
sky news reporting shooter is dead at scene

rip truthteller. u made us proud

bangsaidthegun
shit man. what a guy

thejump
he defo dead? suicide?

Dx99
yeah they just announced on bbc. they said they've
confirmed ID, let's see his face . . .

miguelonthemic
WTF!!!

bangsaidthegun
that is . . . unexpected

Dx99
hooooooooly shit

u guys seeing this?

THERE IS A GIRL.

There is a girl with her face on every newspaper, every news channel. A girl with a grave, defaced.

A girl with blood on her hands.

But once there was a girl who was just a girl.

From the journal of Elise King, entry dated 14th July, 2012

It's all over soon. School, anyway, That might make things better, at least for a while. Six weeks of freedom, and let's not think about what comes after.

Today he came home without his hat. He has to wear his hat because his skin's so sensitive, and it was really, really sunny today, the sunniest it's been all week. His face and his neck were all burnt and angry and red. Mum was still at work so I ran him a cold bath and I rubbed the aftersun on him. I asked him who did it and he wouldn't say because he never says. He tells me everything so I don't know how they make him keep that secret but they do.

When he came downstairs, we watched Dragon Ball Z *and ate ice cream and he pretended he was fine, just like he always does. Why does nobody see it except me? Why does nobody do anything? Last week when he* came home his backpack was all wet and smelled weird. It took me ages to figure out what it was – it was only when he was getting ready for bed and I looked inside and I saw all his books were sludgy green that I knew they'd put his textbooks in the pond.

If Mum actually paid attention, she'd figure it out. All those torn shirts and broken glasses and bruised arms. _She_ thinks it's all from 'being a boy', as if he's climbing trees and hopping fences. Has she actually ever looked at Josh? Does he look like he'd be climbing trees? He's allergic to everything and shy and scared and _wonderful_. He is genuinely the best person I know. _She_ doesn't get to see any of that, because _she_ isn't ever here. She work work works and I look after him. And then she is here, and she doesn't _see_. She doesn't get him, she never has. You'd think she'd have known how special he was, seeing as he came out of her. But she's too busy trying to be perfect, trying to cook us perfect food and create the perfect house and be the perfect mother and pretend that Josh is normal, and that all takes so much time that she forgets to even notice us. It's kind of like she's trying to make it up to us that Dad moved a hundred miles away when they divorced – like we'd rather they'd stayed together and argued the whole time! Like Dad actually paid us any attention when he was here anyway. She's just trying to give us nice things, because she feels guilty about us coming from a broken home or whatever. She's trying *to be a mum and a dad and I feel sorry for her because she doesn't realise we don't need all that. We just need her to be <u>her</u>. Josh needs her.*

But it's all going to be okay. Summer's almost here, and I can take care of him. I'm going to make sure he has the best time ever, and I'm going to find out who's been doing this to him and I WILL MAKE THEM <u>PAY</u>.

Interview with Remy Dixon, 28th September, 2016

It's embarrassing now, when I think about it. I feel, I dunno, ashamed. Because I don't think she actually lied to us about the stuff that happened before she came to Southfield. I reckon we just never asked.

The girls must have, I s'pose. But as far as I was concerned, she shows up in Year 9, a couple of the lads from gym start talking about this hot new girl, and I don't really think anything of it, until Gem and her make friends. To be honest, that was cos she was hot. Gemma was used to being the hot girl in our year, yeah? A new one shows up and she can either make friends with them or be their enemy; friends is the easier option. That sounds harsh but I reckon it's true. That's how Gem thinks.

All I knew was she'd changed schools cos she'd moved in with her dad. She sort of made out it was because she'd fallen out with her mum and we just accepted that, we never asked for details or anything. Not my style. If people want to tell you that kinda private stuff, they will. And she didn't, so: fine.

So. We didn't know any of it. Not then.

What did you say you wanted to know this stuff for? A book?

Well, what kind of book?

No, it ain't that. Thing is, I don't like it how people can make things look a certain way. Like, you can put things in any order you want, yeah? You can make it look like it was our fault, or Eli's. You know what I'm saying? People always tell Eli's story first, like that explains it all. They make it Eli's fault even though he was already gone before it happened. But why not blame it on me and Gem? Why not leave Eli out of it? His face just fits the headline better, right? So people are well up for writing about his devil-worshipping family and his temper and whatever. Don't matter that this probably would've happened anyway.

Right, that day – sorry. So we've just heard about Eli killing himself and Ash has left. Aish is still trying to call him and I'm just sitting there upstairs thinking about how I better call Elise and check how she's doing, still in shock I guess. It sounds weird but all I could think about was this one time, after one of our film nights round at mine, it was just me and Elijah left; the others had all gone home. Thing is, he never really spoke to me, I always got the feeling he didn't really like me, or maybe he was just a bit nervous round me, I don't know. Anyways, we're both just sitting there on the floor, backs to the sofas, and it's still dark from where we were watching the films. In fact, I think I'd turned another one on, some really bad horror that the girls had said we couldn't watch. And after the first couple of minutes, Eli turns to me, and he says, he says, 'I'm scared, Remy.'

And I say, 'Of this? Seriously?'

And he looks at the film and pulls a face and goes, 'No. This is shit.' Which it was.

So I said, 'Okay, I'll change it. But what d'you mean, mate? What you scared of?'

But it was like he'd never said it. I don't know if he just thought better of it, or he'd never meant to say it in the first place, but he pretended like it never happened. He just laughs and goes, 'You want to watch horror, let me show you this Japanese thing,' and took his HDMI out his bag and went to get my laptop. And that was it. We sat up watching films and then he went home. Nothing doing.

But yeah, I was thinking about that night, sitting there at Aish and Ash's house. Thinking about the way he said *I'm scared, Remy.*

Then Aisha comes back up the stairs.

She wasn't crying any more. She was holding her phone, looking all weird, like she couldn't get any words out.

'Is Ash all right?' I said. 'You get through to him?'

And she shook her head. She looked right at me and she said, she said, 'There's something going on at the school.'

THE DAY IS bright and clear and Ash can't bear it. The sunlight bounces off the car bonnets and each beam feels like a blade, each one the knowledge of what has happened to Eli slicing through him again. He can't be still; he can't let it settle. He has to keep moving. His brain likes logic; it likes problems which can be solved and conclusions which can be reached and so it keeps trying to come back to this unthinkable knowledge, trying to process it and package it and draw out its meaning. But he won't let it, he can't let it. He doesn't want this to be a world where Elijah isn't.

Instead, he tries to think ahead. The next hour and the next day and the weeks that will follow. Exams are around the corner; he and Elise have been working hard at revision. He has been worried about Elise, who's suddenly become flippant about the tests, distracted and defensive. He often looks up from his notes to find her staring across the library at people talking or walking or laughing in the playground outside, her eyes narrowed, her pen tapping agitatedly against the desk.

He will go to see her, he decides. He will check on her. *Does she know yet?* he thinks and then he squashes that thought down. He won't think about that, he mustn't think about that. He puts his head down and changes direction.

Elise's house is a twenty-minute walk from the Kapoors' but he manages it in ten. He has long, heron-like legs and he enjoys walking, normally. He likes watching the birds which cluster in the sparse trees around the town, listening to the distant sounds of the motorway and watching planes leave their faint contrails across the sky. The Kapoors have lived in the same semi-detached house, on its long, winding street, since the twins were three, and so they know lots of the people who live there too. Usually when he's walking he's keeping an eye out for people he should wave or nod or say hello to as he passes. But today he keeps his head down, his eyes on the pavement. He concentrates on putting one foot in front of the other, as quickly as possible.

Ash doesn't know much about Elise's father. They live in a big house, in a secluded cul-de-sac, and the car he drives is expensive and changed often. Ash has overheard Gemma making remarks about him being 'dodgy' but has never bothered trying to find out what exactly that means. Gossiping doesn't really interest him and he particularly doesn't like it when his friends are doing it about each other. There was a time once when Ash and Eli showed up at the house with a USB full of *Preacher* comics Elise hadn't read yet, and found some skinny, scared guy banging on the door. When Elise's dad answered the door, he looked like someone Ash would not want staring back at him, his fists clenched like concrete and a vein pulsing at one side of his head. He dragged the small, skinny guy inside, not even noticing the two of them, and Ash had heard him

173

hissing, 'I told you *never* to come here. Do not bring business to my *home*,' before the door to the study slammed shut. But since then, he's seen Mr King only twice – both times while Ash is on his way into the house and Mr King on his way out. Once, he received a nod of the head as the man climbed into his car. The second time, they passed on the shallow front steps. Ash was carrying his physics textbook and three bars of the Millions chocolate Elise liked, and Mr King was carrying a large leather holdall and wearing woollen gloves. Mr King did not say hello or ask how Ash was; instead, he asked a simple question: How is she? Ash thought then that this was extra-caring, a father and daughter reunited after many years apart, and so he just smiled and said, 'She's really good. She's going to ace all of her exams,' because he could only assume that that was everyone's number-one concern.

He turns onto their street, noticing for the first time the silence. No one else around; no birds overhead. He can't even hear the normal faint hum of traffic from the main road behind the thick hedge of fir trees. Elise's house is in the far corner of the cul-de-sac, the only house that's shaded by the firs. The drive is empty, no expensive car in sight. But as Ash gets closer, he sees that the side door is open, gaping like a mouth.

He puts his hand on the handle and stands for a minute, unsure what to do. He has a strange feeling; a kind of crawling in his stomach, and because he doesn't want to address that either, he steps inside and closes the door behind him.

The first thing he notices is the darkness. For a minute he thinks his eyes are struggling to adjust after being out in the sunshine, but as his vision clears he realises that all of the curtains are drawn. There is a stale, dankly sweet smell and he fumbles his way through the kitchen and pulls the blind to reveal a stack of takeaway cartons and foil dishes, all half-full with congealed food, spattered forks sticking out or abandoned on the counter.

As he heads through the dining room and into the lounge, he suddenly realises that he is sneaking through someone else's house and that this isn't really normal, polite behaviour. Everything seems strange and dreamlike; so much of his energy focused on squashing down those thoughts of Elijah, of a tree, of the place beside him on his bed that his friend will no longer occupy.

'Elise?' he tries, opening the curtains a crack. 'Hello?'

The lounge is also untidy; empty cans of beer and cider left on the coffee table and beside one of the chairs, a half-empty bottle of vodka lolling against one of the cushions. A laptop is open on one of the chair's arms. Ash walks over and runs a finger against the trackpad, waking it from hibernation. He frowns at the screen and then picks the laptop up, sitting down on the edge of the sofa with it.

Scrolling back and forth through the screen, he tries to make sense of what he's seeing. He's heard of the message-board 5-star before – he's even visited it in the past for cheat codes for games, for rumours of hidden bonus levels that can be unlocked with the right combination of moves. 5-star is often in the news for also being a place where other, less legal, things are shared: porn, drugs, hacked sites. He can't imagine why Elise would be on here. Especially on this board; he frowns as he reads over the posts again. Message after message filled with hatred about popular kids at different schools, all of them talking about mean girls and jocks and how they should pay. About how the 'betas', the losers and the geeks, will have their day.

He reaches the last couple of posts on the board, the warnings from 'truth_teller' about a shooting at a UK school. When he sees the discussion of *where* in the UK, his heart begins to pound. The beginnings of another piece of knowledge start knitting themselves together in his brain, fluttering their way into life, but it's another thing he isn't ready to process and so he pushes the laptop away and runs up the stairs.

He's never been in Elise's room before. Because her dad's so often away, they've always hung out downstairs, the six of them spread out across the lounge and the kitchen, acting like it's their own house. In the darkened hallway, he can't remember which door is hers. He opens three – a bathroom, two neat guestrooms – before he finds it. He knows immediately that it's hers; her familiar grey blanket scarf hanging from the desk chair, a framed certificate on the wall. The bed is unmade, deep purple sheets mussed up. The knowledge begins to spread its wings properly, begins batting against the edges of his mind, trying to get his attention. *What did you do?* he thinks, acid rising up his throat, and he isn't sure if he is thinking of Elise or Elijah.

Open on the desk is a notebook, and he takes a step closer, sees the rows of rushed, irregular writing, the way the ink bleeds across the letters. He reaches out to pick it up, tentatively as if it might be hot.

When he sees what is written there, he runs.

He doesn't even stop to close the open side door behind him.

From the journal of Elise King, entry dated 15th October, 2012

I am in trouble.

<u>*BIG*</u> *trouble.*

His name is Devon. He has brown eyes and curly hair and he laughs like he's never going to stop.

He doesn't even know I exist.

Being in Year 8 is okay I guess. I like some of my teachers better than last year. I still hang around with Rosie and Zaira. I joined Dance Club so sometimes the girls from there talk to me. Mr Jahdav is still trying to persuade me to join Maths Society and I guess I might. He's really nice and I like maths plus you get to go on trips to compete with other schools.

Mum has a new boyfriend. His name is Gareth and she brought him home over summer to meet us. He seems okay. He took us to the cinema once, and then the four of us went out to TGI Fridays for dinner another time. Now he stays over all the time, but he cooks sometimes so that's not so bad. They go out a lot too, but he always gives us money to order pizza or sometimes Chinese. Josh likes pizza best so usually I let him pick. It's good for Josh to have a guy around who's interested in what he has to say. He was only six when Dad left so I don't think he even remembers him that well, but I know Josh sort of freaked Dad out. Dad wanted a son he could take to boxing and football, he doesn't really do talking or art or the things Josh likes. Gareth tries at least.

Things are getting worse for Josh. He hasn't said anything but I can tell. I kind of hoped him starting Year 7 would make it better, like maybe the kids would forget about him or get bored or whatever. But that hasn't happened. If anything I think it's got worse. The other day he was limping when he came home. I sneaked upstairs and looked through the gap in his door when he was getting changed and he had bruises all down his side. I tried asking him about it but as usual he told me he bumped into a door. He can't even look me in the eye when he says it, like he's afraid to.

But now he's at the same school as me I can really do something about it. I can find out who they are, and I can make them stop. I will stop them hurting him. I'll do whatever it takes.

Interview with Aisha Kapoor, 28th September, 2016

I heard it on the radio, when I'd gone downstairs to try and call Ash – I just needed to keep moving, I couldn't sit down, I couldn't breathe properly. I can't really describe it but it just felt like everything was unravelling, it felt like there was this big black cloud rolling closer and closer and something terrible was going to happen. I know that sounds weird now, with everything that happened, but—

Sorry. I just need a second.

It's difficult, remembering, you know?

Is that the word, foreboding? Yes, I guess that was what it was then; at the time I didn't have a name for it or anything. It was just *there*. I was listening to the phone ring and waiting for Ash to pick up and I walked into the kitchen. The radio was on from where Ash had been making breakfast, before we heard – it was the news, I think, or at least people were talking.

I remember really clearly that the phone stopped ringing. You know how it does, when someone doesn't pick up? And it just kind of beeps at you and stops trying? And I didn't even notice then, because I was too busy listening to the radio, this breaking-news thing they were saying, like something out of a film. I can still hear the man's voice now, I can still remember standing there listening to him. 'We're hearing that there's a possible hostage situation over at Southfield School, after reports of gunfire on the premises.' That's what he said. Can you imagine hearing that, how strange it felt? It took me a minute to actually process it, and then I started shaking.

Um, that's when I went upstairs to find Remy.

THE SCHOOL IS dark and she is prepared. She found the fuse-box easily; she remembers each and every time they passed it and Elijah pointed it out to her, the same way he did with everything: That's where the power comes from. Those trees will never lose their leaves. That type of car isn't made any more. This is the way the world works.

She has to move quickly now; people will soon come to investigate the power cut and she must strike first, she must keep them where they are. But she is the fastest runner in her year and she is prepared.

She loops the chain through the handles of the doors and padlocks it tight. The side entrance to the school is already safely locked in the same way; she made sure of that on her way in. One more set and then the school is secure; they are all in this together and she will end things the way they should be ended.

She watches her hands move over the chains and is amazed at how smoothly they do, how easy it is to make each step. She doesn't shake, she doesn't falter.

This is the way things should be.

This is the way things must be.

She takes the gun from her pocket and tests its weight in her hand.

The first footsteps come towards her.

From the journal of Elise King, entry dated 2nd November, 2012

He. Spoke. To. Me.

Oh my God. It was the <u>best</u> *thing ever. He came right up to me at lunchtime and said, 'Hey, you're in Maths Society, right?' And I got nervous, like he was going to tease me, but I tried not to go red and I just said yes.*

He said, 'Oh cool. Hey, I am too, I just missed the first session. So are you coming to the competition at Roehawk High next month?'

I nodded and he smiled and said, 'Cool. Well, catch you later.' And then he got up off the bench and went off to join the queue for food. Rosie and Zaira were <u>dying</u>. *It was amazing.*

Now I just have to really study so I can impress him when we beat Roehawk in the competition. If we do, we get to go to the county championships!

The rest of the day wasn't so great. I keep telling Josh to come sit with me at lunch, and to walk home with me, and sometimes he does, but sometimes he doesn't show. And sometimes I have to go to Dance Club or Maths Society so I tell him to wait for me but he doesn't, and those are always the days when he's limping or missing part of his uniform or his books or whatever. Today at lunch he didn't turn up in the canteen, so after the whole thing with Devon I made an excuse to Rosie and Zai and I went to look for him.

I checked everywhere. I went round the playground, and up on the school field even though we're not supposed to go up there till summer term, and then I checked the nurse's office and the classroom where sometimes they have Homework Club at lunch.

I'd pretty much given up and was heading back to the canteen when I saw him coming out of the boys' toilets in Oak Block. I was right behind him and I reached out and touched his head, because he's still so small, so much smaller than me. His hair was damp but really hot, like it'd been under the hand dryer, and I could see there were splashes all over his blazer and his shirt collar.

When I touched him, he freaked, like jumped back and kind of curled into himself, like I was about to hit him. It made me want to cry, right there in the corridor. But I just put my arm round him and I said, 'What you doing out here?' even though I could see for myself that they'd held his head in the toilet, I could still see the *finger marks on the back of his neck. I just said, 'Come get some food with me,' and I took him into the canteen.*

I need to be smarter. I need to find evidence. I need to make sure these kids don't get away with this.

Interview with Julie Wu, 23rd September, 2016

It was just a normal day. I had not heard about Elijah. Perhaps on another day of the week I might have, but on Thursdays we did not have a staff morning meeting – there was a committee meeting instead which most teachers did not have to attend. I'm sure that it would have been announced to the staff during lunch, if things had been different. Of course that was too late.

I had a Year 8 biology lesson first period and then admin time during second, so I was in the staff room marking my Year 10 essays ready for my class after break. That was not like me; I preferred not to mark work during school hours as it was difficult to concentrate. Southfield was always loud. But I'd been unable to finish these essays the evening before, and in fact that second period was unusually quiet. The staff room looks out over the playground and I remember sitting there, watching the clouds race across the sky. There was an unsettled feeling everywhere, though perhaps that is something I'm remembering because of what happened. I'm not sure.

It must have been about fifteen minutes into second period when I heard the first scream. It sounded distant, and when I went to the window I couldn't see anybody there. There was a bang then but that didn't immediately alarm me. Children are quite often setting off fireworks and things in the woodland behind the school. And the sound was more muffled than that; it sounded almost like a car backfiring. I went back to my table and carried on with what I was doing.

It must have been about five or ten minutes later that the phone in the staff room started to ring. At that exact moment I heard another bang, except it was louder this time, and sounded more like it was coming from somewhere closer by. I think it was then that I started to worry. That phone is so rarely used I don't think I had ever heard it ring before. I remember for a second that I did not want to answer. I was afraid, but I did not understand why. I reached out and picked it up and then I heard more screams coming from down the hall.

It was the receptionist, Uri.

Oh, he was screaming, just screaming. 'There's a shooter in the school!'

I didn't understand, I asked him to repeat himself. But then there was another bang, more screams. I went to the door of the staff room and I looked out through the porthole and I saw a girl lying on the floor, facedown. And a figure coming down the hall towards me, a gun in hand. They had a hood pulled up and the lights in the hall had gone off so I could not see their face, but when they were closer I thought that I recognised the jumper – it had a design down one arm and I knew that I had seen Elijah wearing it. So, of course – I thought . . .

I ducked down. The door to the staff room locks and it was dark inside with the clouds covering the sun. So I pressed myself against the door in case he looked in and I found my phone in my pocket. I dialled 999.

HE RUNS LIKE he's never run before. His feet hit the pavement at odd angles, his arms pump back and forth with hands extended as if he can claw his way through the air. He stumbles a couple of times, loose stones on the road's surface spraying out from under his feet. Drivers hit their horns angrily at him as he dashes across junctions without looking, without caring.

And all the time, he thinks of the words scratched into that blank page.

He is gone.

They must pay.

He falls properly this time, hitting the pavement with arms outstretched, his chest breaking the fall and the air knocked out of him.

I have the gun.

Dazed, he pushes himself up to hands and knees, clambers to his feet. His palms are bleeding and he brushes gravel from the cuts before remembering where he is, where he's going. He starts to run again, and a new pain shooting up his shin reminds him with every step how much further there is to go. He hopes he's wrong; he hopes this is all a miscalculation, an adding-up of evidence that has gone fundamentally wrong.

But deep down, he knows. He isn't wrong. Something terrible is about to happen.

Something terrible has already happened.

Elijah Elijah Elijah. The pain in his leg is vicious and right, and for a second he just wants to keep running. He wants to run on and on until the pain is all he can think about, until all his other thoughts are drowned out. He wants to run until he can escape. But one thought keeps repeating, one sentence scratched onto a notebook page.

They must pay.

He turns left onto Rugby Street. The school looms ahead.

And then he stops again. He realises his mistake; he realises the thing that any of the others – Aisha, Remy, Gemma – would have done first. He fumbles his phone from his pocket. Finds her number, hits 'Call'. Listens to it ring, the tones stretching on and on and on. He suddenly thinks that this is the first thing he should have done anyway – that as soon as he got the call this morning he should have called Elise, the only other person who was perhaps as close to Elijah as he was (the only other person who might really understand). And the thinking of that thought is the final brick that pulls the wall down; he remembers the call from Elijah's mum, the way she was crying, how the words were barely understandable. He puts it all together, the words and the thoughts and the memories and he sees Elijah, his friend, making a decision that will change everything forever, and he realises that he's really gone.

And then, in a chain-reaction of thought after thought, the phone still ringing, he realises that Elise probably received a call before he did, that Eli's mum has probably seen Elise in their house, has heard Eli talk about Elise, far more than she has Ash recently.

The phone cuts out; call not answered. He starts to run again.

At the school, he sees the flashing lights, the people starting to mill around the gates. A car shoots by him way too fast and then stops up ahead. He watches as it parks lopsidedly by the kerb; the driver's door flies open and a man climbs awkwardly out with a huge camera round his neck and a case full of other equipment, a phone pressed to his ear. And Ash knows for sure; he knows. Something bad has happened; something bad is happening *right now*.

So he doesn't bother trying to get into school through the Rugby Street side entrance or the main gates. He doubles back and runs around the edge of the school. There's a dusty footpath about halfway down Rugby Street which nobody ever really uses unless they want to have a sneaky smoke before or after school, and he ducks down it, hurrying down the part which is tree-lined and shady, until the back of the school comes into view. He's always been quick-thinking like this – always able to adapt and adjust a plan as new information arises. It's a simple chain of thought for him: the police are at the school; there is a gun inside; they will shut down the exits. And so he needs to find a new way inside.

Finally, the path widens out, the trees older and bigger here. He knows exactly the place he's looking for, and he stops just short of it, trying to catch his breath. He leans against the chain-link fence which runs the whole way round the school and looks up at this very particular point where one of the silvering old trees looms up and over the footpath, several of its branches sending their shadows past the fence and onto the school grounds. He stays there a second too long, trying to catch his breath, his heart kicking so hard he's afraid it'll burst right out of his ribs. He looks up at the tree, at its wide and cracking branches. He's seen Remy do this plenty of times, when a football has cleared the fence and he's volunteered to retrieve it – each time he was boosted over the fence by others and then he clambered back over by himself, making it look easy. Ash *thinks* Remy weighs more than him, so surely he'll be able to heave himself up onto that same branch, surely he'll be over the fence in a second.

Of course, the loud and annoying logic centre in his brain is quick to remind him that Remy is a gymnast, that Remy is used to holding his entire weight on a fingertip, basically, and that all of his muscles are just waiting there, ready to be called on whenever they're needed. So Ash can't really assume that anything Remy makes look easy is *actually* easy. He looks up at the tree; its branches suddenly seem ridiculously thin, its trunk stupidly slippery.

But then he hears a shot from the school behind him. And he knows, right then, that he doesn't have time to think about things any more. He pushes up his sleeves and jumps at the trunk, sliding clumsily back down it the first time but finding foot- and hand-holds the second. He pulls himself up into the branches, ignoring the pain in his already skinned hands.

He feels a weird sort of excitement, once he's actually up in the tree, and he wants to yell out to someone. *Hey! Look at me! I climbed a tree!* Just like a little kid. He wants someone to tell him how well he's done, how strong he is. Because he doesn't feel strong right now.

But that shot rings on in his ears and so he knows he has to keep going. His muscles creak as he shifts himself under one of the broad branches – the effort of hanging there almost too much for his spindly arms. The branch bends and he knows he has to move fast.

He is almost two feet out from the trunk of the tree, almost at the point where the branch starts to become more of a twig. Sweat beads on his back and he tries to tell himself he's almost there. He glances beneath him and realises that this is almost true – he's inches from the fence now. But the branch thins out dramatically and his swelling hands are beginning to lose their grip. He grips the branch tighter with his knees and as he does, he feels his phone falling from his pocket, hears it thud on the ground below. He doesn't stop; no time to go back for it. The branch makes an ominous cracking sound, just as he realises he is over the fence, and in his surprise, he lets go, falling awkwardly. He lands on one ankle, the rest of his body toppling over it, and doesn't stop to see if he's injured. He clambers straight back up and hobbles quickly towards the shade of the school, ignoring the spiteful twinge shooting up his ankle with every step.

There are no exits on this side of the school, but Ash isn't looking for one anyway. The part of his brain that wasn't engaged in keeping him hanging from that tree has already been probing the layout of the school, trying to figure out the best way in, and so he knows exactly where he's going he doesn't hesitate. He looks for the window he needs. A hundred feet on, in an alcove of the building, he finds it: the boys' bathroom in the technology wing of the school. Nobody ever uses it, because it's sort of tucked away (you almost can't see it from the main corridor) and none of the maintenance staff ever seem to go near it, so it's pretty disgusting. And, more importantly, he knows that one of its windows doesn't quite fit its frame – in winter, icy wind whistles through the place, making it even less appealing.

In the end, he doesn't even need to force it; it's another hot day and someone has already propped the window ajar. He slides his long pianist's fingers into the gap until he finds the arm, pushes it from its post and gently lets the window swing open. He thinks he can hear the distant thundering of a helicopter and he glances around before putting both hands on the sill and heaving himself up, one knee braced against the bricks as the other leg unfolds awkwardly into the room. He almost tumbles again but manages to grab the edge of the urinal just in time, lowering himself the rest of the way.

He leaves the window open. He has a horrible, churning feeling that ways in and out of the school might be limited.

He allows himself a couple of seconds to catch his breath, standing in the dank bathroom, rubbing the bleeding palms of his hands against his T-shirt.

And then he opens the door and steps into the school.

From the journal of Elise King, entry dated 12th December, 2012

I had them. I was sure I had them.

I had to be clever about it. So I waited after school. I hid behind the caretaker's car, which was parked on his drive right at the top of the road down to school. Everyone has to go past his house, no matter where they live. That's the only way in or out of the place.

So I hid, and I felt sick. I had my phone in my hand ready, the camera on.

It had got so much worse. He had bruises on his face, his books were all torn up, and still he wouldn't say anything. One day last week I begged him to tell me so I could make it stop, I begged him till I cried, but he just sat there and shook his head and I could see he was crying too, but when I tried to hug him he just pushed me away and ran up to his room.

So I waited. I watched all of the kids stream past, laughing and talking and shoving each other, like some kind of stampede. I watched how all the girls stared at each other when they didn't know they were being watched, sizing each other up. I watched the boys jump on each other and call each other names, smiling smiling smiling. And then it got quieter, and there were less and less of them. My knees were kind of hurting from kneeling on the gravel, but I kept very still. I was supposed to be in Dance Club, and I knew Josh knew that, so I figured he'd try and hide, wait to walk home on his own after everyone else had already left.

And I knew that they wouldn't let him.

When everyone had gone and there was silence, I finally heard his footsteps. And I kept very very still and I watched him hurry past, his head down and his hands tucked up under his armpits with his fingers locked round the straps of his backpack.

And just like I knew they would, they followed him.

Three of them, shirts pulled loose and iron-shiny trousers with scuffed cuffs. Two girls and a boy. I watched them watching him, whispering. I edged my way out on the gravel, slowly, slowly, not caring if it cut me. When I got to the edge of the drive, I saw Josh peeping back over his shoulder. He'd spotted them following him, and he started walking faster, trying to get to the bottom of the street, where the main road is, where there are people.

One of the boys picked up a rock and threw it at him. It bounced off the back of his head and it must have really hurt. My hands were shaking as I filmed them. The road seemed so, so long. And they were so much taller than him, even though they were only his age. They caught up to him easily. I started walking faster, trying to keep up with them. I just wanted to get them on camera, I just wanted to have something I could show to the teachers, and to Mum, so they'd realise, so they'd do something. I wanted to get them expelled.

'Where you going, Joshy?' one of the girls said, and she was close enough to kick him in the back of the leg so that his knee buckled and he almost fell.

I hid in a gap in the bushes and my heart was beating so fast I thought it might burst. This was the plan but it was so <u>hard</u> just watching, I wanted to do something. But I had to keep telling myself, Just a little bit longer, just to make sure I had enough to make sure they got what they deserved.

'Yeah, Josh,' one of the boys said, and he grabbed Josh by the back of his collar and lifted him right off the ground. 'Don't you want to stay and talk?' He threw him into the hedge and Josh's glasses came off and I could see that Josh was stammering which he only does when he's really nervous or afraid.

And I couldn't take it any more.

The other girl leaned forward and pinched his cheeks so his face was all squished up and he was going red and stammering and I could see the first tears in the corners of his eyes.

And I couldn't take it any more.

I pulled her by the hair. I punched the boy in the face. I punched the girl in the face. Someone hit me, someone punched me, but none of that mattered.

They ran away and I wanted to hit them more.

Interview with Remy Dixon, 28th September, 2016

I didn't really get it at first. When Aish said something was going on at the school, I thought she meant to do with Elijah. And then she's trying to phone Ash again, saying something about someone getting shot. In the end I had to go right up to her and take the phone away and get her to explain properly, yeah? She just took me downstairs to listen to the radio.

They were saying that someone had been shooting a gun inside the school. That's not exactly the kind of thing you expect to hear round here. This ain't London, there ain't nobody carrying weapons or anything like that.

What, did I know it was Elise? I ask myself that all the time. Sometimes I think yeah, I did. Sometimes I remember looking at Aish and I can actually *remember* looking at her thinking *It's Elise, oh my God, it's Elise*. But I don't think that's true. I just think that's cos of everything we know now. Memory's pretty screwed up like that, isn't it? It's changing the whole time. It upgrades itself without you noticing.

Look, I think right then I didn't think anything much except 'Gun equals bad'. My first question was where Ash was, because I had Aish in front of me, bawling her eyes out. I was pretty sure he'd gone to see Elise. I still think that – that's what he would've done. He'd have realised how much the news would have messed with her head; he'd have gone round to help her. That was what Ash was like. Caring. So I weren't worried about him. Not right then anyways. I told Aisha that. I tried to calm her down.

Nah, it was Aisha who said we should go to the school. She got all pale and said, 'Gem might be there,' and that's when we started walking. We just left the house and started walking to school. The whole way there Aisha's looking at Twitter, trying to figure out what's going on. No one seemed to know, it was just the same stuff that had been on the radio being retweeted all the time. 'Omg shots fired at Southside!' 'Can't get anywhere near Southside, police have got a cordon all the way round!', that kinda thing. There was some more specific stuff which was harder; I remember reading these tweets about how it was a teacher who'd made the 999 call. I remember thinking about which teacher it could've been the whole way up to the school, stupid things like that. And then all this stuff about armed police on their way. It didn't feel real.

When we got near the school, we could see the helicopter. I dunno if it was a police one or a news one. We weren't saying much, me and Aish. Like I said, it didn't seem real. I felt like I was in a dream or something. I kept trying to call Gem but her phone was off. That same old voicemail message every time. Her battery was always dying, it wasn't exactly unusual. I didn't think anything of it at the time.

We got to the end of Rugby Street and there was police tape and cones and shit. There was just one officer there – I saw later that most of them were round at the front entrance, and out the back – and he looked fucking terrified, to be honest. He looked like he didn't have a clue what he was doing.

'You can't go past here, guys,' he goes, like he's a bouncer or something. But he was all sweaty and his voice was kinda shaking.

Aish asked him what was happening and he kind of looked around, like he was hoping someone would give him the answer or something. 'I can't say anything,' he kept saying, but Aisha weren't having any of it.

'What's going on? Someone has a gun? Is it a student? Have people been hurt?' She just kept on throwing questions at him until the guy looked like he was going to cry or punch her. It was only when he got his radio and threatened to have us arrested that we backed off.

We got back to the end of the road and we looked at each other like, 'What do we do now?'

SHE MOVES THROUGH the hallways, a shadow, her fingers trailing against the lockers. She glances through classroom windows, sees the hurried efforts to get under desks, the frightened teachers trying to remember their training. She wants to laugh.

She wants to scream.

She doesn't make a sound.

The noise inside her head is almost too much to bear; thoughts of their laughing faces, of the words they all typed, spin round and round and grow louder and louder, buzzing bees in her brain.

She doesn't make a sound, and she will silence them too. One by one, she will silence them.

He comes to her; she doesn't have to find him. He comes running round the corner with two girls from their science class, and slides to a cartoonish stop when he sees her.

'Elise—' he starts (she doesn't think Derran has ever even said her name before) and then he sees the gun and she remembers the gun and he turns and she shoots him. She looks at the screaming girl beside him. She doesn't remember her name, can't really place her face because their faces are all the same, these *Bellas*, these bitches, these laughing, lipsticked mouths, and before she's really thought about it at all, she shoots her too.

She lets the other girl run.

She is so very tired.

From the journal of Elise King, entry dated 15th December, 2012

Their names are Olivia Hall, Will Johnson and Priti Malik. I know that because the Head told me.

My phone got smashed in the fight so I didn't have the video but I didn't care. I was going to tell on them anyway. I had to make it stop.

But they told first. They told their parents and their parents told the Head that I attacked them. And now it's my word against theirs.

The worst thing is that Josh won't say anything, even with me on his side. He's even <u>angry</u> at me, he says I've made things worse. I tell him that if we tell, we can make it all go away, but he says that they say if he tells they will burn our house down. Guess who he believes more?

I tried to tell Mum but she talked to Josh and she said I was overreacting. She says if he says he's fine, he is. She doesn't get that they got to him. I don't know how she can't see it, it's written all over him. But she just wants to carry on with her happy new life with Gareth, where everything is shiny and lovely and her kids don't actually need anything from her. Urgh.

The Head was quite kind to me. She said they would keep an eye on things, make sure Josh was okay. She said maybe I'd got the wrong idea, and that probably it was just a silly falling about between them all. But she said it was wrong of me to do what I did. She put me in detention for two whole weeks.

Olivia Hall has a sister in Year 9. I know that because she waited for me after detention yesterday. She punched me in the stomach so I couldn't breathe, and she told me if I went near her sister again, she would kill me.

She can do what she wants to me. I don't care. But nobody's going to hurt Josh again. Nobody.

Interview with Aisha Kapoor, 28th September, 2016

So we ended up at the main entrance to school, you know, up on Queen Street? There were lots of people up there, and the police were there, trying to keep everyone back and stuff. The school gates had been closed and there were police cars in front of the school and lots of officers walking around in bulletproof vests and helmets. People were crying but nobody really seemed to know what was going on so I kept on checking my phone, seeing what people were saying on Twitter. The local radio station was tweeting updates but they were all like the same kind of thing: *Identity of the shooter currently unknown, police are on the scene*, just nothingy stuff, you know? Oh, and there were kids claiming to be inside the school but I think they found out afterwards that a lot of that was people messing around.

I remember seeing this one in particular, it's always stayed in my head how I felt when I saw it. This boy had tweeted 'Kid with a dragon hoody walking down hall with a gun. Teacher locked us in the classroom'. And that made me go cold all over, because it was Elijah who had a dragon hoody. Black with gold down the sleeves, making those swirly, pretty Chinese dragons, you know the ones? And for a second, I thought Ash had got it really, really wrong – I thought that Elijah wasn't dead, and then I started thinking about ghosts and revenge, all this crazy, crazy stuff. I was so confused, that whole day felt like some horrible nightmare, like nothing made any sense. I couldn't stop all these awful thoughts going through my head.

I remember showing Remy that tweet, and his face going all weird, because I guess he was thinking the same thing as me.

And then we heard another shot.

*From the journal of Elise King, entry dated 12th
January, 2013*

A new year, a new everything.

*Josh seems so much happier, so much more himself. He
laughs all the time, he comes home and he strolls in
smiling and the horrible squeezing feeling in my chest
has started to go away.*

Maybe it's over. Maybe I made it go away.

*Mum and Gareth got engaged on New Year's Eve. That's
okay, I guess. He's nice even if he isn't very interesting.
He paints walls in the house and he buys new shelves
and he asks us questions about our day. I like that part
about him. He at least pretends to be interested in what
we're doing. He doesn't have to. And he cooks too, he
cooks all of the things Josh likes best and he asks me
what I like too, but I just say the same things as Josh so
he'll make those all the time.*

And then today, something even better. At break-time, Devon came up to me. He told me how well I did at the Maths Society contest at Roehawk. He asked me if I wanted to study together for the county championships we're going to at some school in Birmingham. He took my number.

MY NUMBER!

This will be a new year for all of us.

From the journal of Elise King, entry dated 15th January, 2013

When I look at that last entry, I want to tear it right out.

How could I ever think things were going to get better? How could I ever think that maybe, <u>maybe</u>, things were going to be okay for us?

Mum and Gareth keep going away. Sometimes for a night, sometimes for two. He says that I'm old enough to look after Josh by myself, and that's true, but Mum usually makes Mrs Gregg next door pop in and check up on us. But I don't know how to tell Mum that right now we need her.

It happened again. I <u>saw</u> them. After school, Olivia and Priti, throwing stones at Josh's head. They followed him right down the street and I followed <u>them</u>. I threw stones at <u>them</u>. Priti ran away but Olivia just looked at me and laughed.

So I hurt her. She DESERVED it.

And then Orla, her sister, waited for <u>me</u> after school. Her friends held me down and she punched me five times in the face.

I didn't cry. I didn't do anything. I just waited for them to let me go and then I went home to make sure Josh was okay.

The website went up yesterday. The first thing I heard about it was on Facebook. Some kid in my form posted the link and I guess he forgot we were friends because I saw it. 'The Truth About the Kings' is what it says but it's nothing so clever as that. It's just a whole page full of ugly photos of me, of Joshy, of Mum. I don't even know where they found them all, it must have taken a long time. A lot of Googling. There's Mum at some prize-giving for local businesses, and she must have blinked at the wrong time because her eyes are half-rolled back in her head. But whoever made the page has added in a joint, some smudgy Microsoft Paint smoke spiralling away from it.

I don't think my mum has ever even <u>seen</u> weed, let alone smoked it. But it's a bad photo. I guess it's kind of funny. It's creative at least.

But then there's the photos of me and Josh. Some of them are pictures people have taken from my Facebook. I only got it a couple of months ago and I didn't know that I hadn't set the privacy settings right, that everyone could see them if they wanted. They picked the least flattering ones, obviously, or the embarrassing ones, like me at my birthday two years ago with chocolate cake smeared all round my mouth.

What's worse is that some of them are recent, and I don't know who took them. They're of us walking to school, at lunch, at break. There's one of me buttoning up my shirt, taken through my bedroom window. The caption says <u>GET SOME TITS</u>. There's one of Josh looking out of his window, with that dreamy look he gets sometimes when he's thinking. They've scrawled <u>WINDOWLICKER</u> above his head.

I keep meaning to report it. But I can't stop watching the comments appearing. 'So fucking ugly' they keep writing under photos of me. 'Little retard' someone writes under a photo of Josh dropping some of the filling out of his sandwich one lunchtime. There's a picture of the two of us leaving school one day, walking home together. I've got my arm round him and the commenters underneath think that's disgusting. 'VOM!' one of them has written. 'Well, nobody else will shag her,' someone else has put, 'guess she has to settle for her brother.' Every time I look at all of the words that keep appearing, over and over, my face gets really hot and I feel like I can't breathe. But I can't stop watching.

Today when I went to our usual table at lunch, Rosie gave me a funny look. 'Do you mind, erm . . . maybe sitting that way a bit?' she said, pointing at the opposite side of the table. 'Why?' I asked, putting my tray down even though I didn't feel hungry any more. 'Well, it's just . . .' Zai couldn't even look at me while she was speaking. 'We're in the photos too. I don't want pictures of me stuffing my face on the internet.' 'Yeah,' Rosie said. 'At least if you sit there, we won't be in shot.'

I left my food there and went out and sat in the library by myself. Nobody spoke to me. It's like I have a disease, like people are afraid unpopularity is catching.

It'll all blow over. They'll get bored soon.

Interview with Julie Wu, 23rd September, 2016

I don't know how long I sat on the floor, shaking. The 999 operator told me to stay on the phone. She kept repeating it, over and over. *Stay on the phone. Keep talking to me.* She wanted me to tell her what was happening, but there was nothing, there was just silence. She told me to stay there, to stay where I was safe, but how could I? There were students out in the hallway; I had heard shots. I had to go and see. I had to try to help.

I stood up and I checked through the small porthole window in the staffroom door. There was no movement from the corridor. The girl was lying on the floor still but I thought that perhaps her hand had changed position. There was another person sitting against the wall – sitting isn't the right word; he was slumped there. He was a boy from my Year 11 class.

Yes, Derran.

When I saw him, I ran out. I went straight to him and I tried to wake him. He was alive, he was moaning but very, very quietly. He'd been shot in the shoulder and blood was running down his arm and onto the floor. I pressed my hand to it and I tried to get him to open his eyes. He was sweating and his skin had turned almost grey. But I managed to get him to look at me, I managed to get him to sit up a little.

It's like they say – you become very strong in a situation like that, you can do things you would not be able to on a normal day. I got Derran's arm round my neck and I got him onto his feet. 'Walk with me,' I kept saying to him, 'stay with me.' And he managed to shuffle along, leaning on me. He had his eyes closed and his head was drooping but I managed to get him into the staff room. I sat him down in the corner, where he couldn't be seen from the door, and then I went back, to the girl.

She'd been shot in the back. I didn't know her. She had a pulse but it was weak. She was smaller than Derran so I could carry her. I took her into the staffroom too and I locked the door behind us. I kept the lights off and I picked up my phone and the operator was still on the line. There were more bangs then, but they were coming from the second floor.

ASH WALKS QUICKLY through deserted corridors, trying to keep his footsteps as light and as silent as possible. Every squeak of his trainers against the linoleum makes him wince. But he knows he has to go faster.

He's walked through these hallways so many times since he started in Year 7, almost five years ago. He's made friends and he's had ideas and those ideas have changed; they're still changing. Before this morning, his biggest worry has been about what to do next. Everyone expects him to study forever, to become an expert on something, to some day give lectures and write theses. But he doesn't know if that's what he wants. He doesn't know if that will be enough.

He and Elijah have talked about bigger things, about changing things, about making things better for people. He feels hope when he thinks of these things, although it's mostly shapeless, an unformed idea that sometimes means going into politics, sometimes means creating art: novels, plays, paintings, all of the things that make him *feel* when he's built his walls of logic too high to escape them. *Close your eyes*, Elijah would say sometimes when he played a piece of music for Ash. *Close your eyes and* listen.

Elijah. Elijah decided things would never get better for *him*. When Ash thinks this, it's almost like a physical hole inside him; he wants to stuff a hand inside it. Because he failed, he failed at what he thinks must be the most basic role of being a friend: he couldn't persuade Eli that there was something worth living for.

He reaches the main atrium, where the reception desk and the front doors are. He isn't surprised to find these locked, and he remembers with a chill the message from the user 'killer_kenny' on that open message board on Elise's laptop. *slow the police down.*

The room is dark, the glass of the doors tinted, and he turns slowly, letting his eyes adjust. The receptionist is flopped across the desk. His pale blue shirt is black with blood. Ash has to hold onto the wall to stop himself from crumpling.

Up until now, a tiny, stubborn part of him has been harbouring a hope that this is all a misunderstanding, that he has got it all wrong. This is Elise, after all. His friend. A person he thought he knew.

And yet here it is in front of him, the receptionist, Uri, a guy they all know and like, sprawled across the desk with his arms at odd angles. Ash thinks, with a sickening lurch of his stomach, of Aisha's ragdoll when they were kids, the way it would be dropped and forgotten when their mother called them for dinner.

But then he takes a deep breath, he lets the calm wash over him. He goes to Uri and he checks his pulse; he confirms what he already knows. He wants to move him; he wants to make things better, give him a respectful position to wait in.

But the calm tells him that he can't. The calm tells him that everything must be left as it is; all the pieces of this fractured day must be left for the people who need to understand to put back together and assemble as a whole.

He carries on down the hall.

From the journal of Elise King, entry dated 4th February, 2013

I tried. I did try.

When Mum and Gareth got back from their weekend in the Cotswolds, I showed them the website. Mum tried to laugh it off – until she found the photos of her. They'd added more by then, horrible, unflattering ones from the 80s that they must have found online. Then she saw the things that had been written about Josh, the things that called him a retard, spaz, a windowlicker. And her face got really red and she didn't say anything else. The next morning she marched into school with us and we sat in the Head's office while the Head looked at all the things that had been said about us.

They'd investigate, she said. Our school does not tolerate bullying.

The website disappeared for a while, but they couldn't find out who'd set it up. I think it was Olivia Hall's sister, Orla, and her stupid boyfriend Jackson. They shove into me whenever they see me around school and sometimes they follow me whispering and laughing.

It doesn't really matter who set it up now. Hurting us has become the new school sport. Feet stick out in every crowded corridor to trip me up, people point phones at me wherever I go, hoping to get the next ugly photo to put on the next website or to post on Facebook for everyone to like.

I don't have friends any more. Zaira and Rosie stuck around for a while but I can't blame them for wanting to get away from me. If you walk places with me, you get stuff thrown at you (pens and books hurt but at least they don't stain like squished-up sandwiches or too-soft fruit). If you sit with me at lunch, you get your photo taken, you get bits of mashed potato or ketchup or jelly flicked at you from spoons. You get people laughing at you, staring at you all the time. You get people shouting stuff at you, pushing you, kicking you, pinching the soft flesh of your arms as you try to get past them in the busy corridors. Why would anyone want to go through that if they don't have to?

This sounds stupid but it hurts me more when other people ignore me. Yesterday, I was standing outside the netball courts, waiting for P.E. (I'd been clever and got changed at lunchtime so I wouldn't have to go to the changing rooms where no teachers can see us) when Orla and her friends came along. I almost thought they might just walk past me but obviously that would never actually happen.

They grabbed me. One of them – the redhead one, I don't know her name but she's pretty and she's usually gentle, I feel like she doesn't really want to hurt me, she always almost looks sorry – got my arms behind my back, while the sharp-faced blonde one pushed me down to the ground and sat on my legs. Orla just took her time. She took out a lighter and she held it <u>just</u> close enough to my ears to sting. She ran it along the edge of my cheek. They laughed. They all laughed.

The worst part is that when they finally let me up, all of my face hot but not burnt enough to show (they're too smart for that, at least for now), there were people all around us. My whole P.E. class, just waiting for netball, pretending not to see. A couple of boys, getting rugby equipment out of the supply shed. A couple of boys and him. Devon. I stood up with my legs all shaky and he looked right at me and he didn't do anything at all. He didn't smile or wave. He didn't stop them when I was on the ground. He pretended like he didn't even see me.

Just like they all pretend that they don't see me.

I don't care. I don't care I don't care I don't care. If doing that stuff to me meant they weren't doing it to

Josh, I'd ask for more. I'd take the photos myself, I'd elbow myself in the side and kick myself in the shin and save them all the effort.

But it doesn't. They sing songs about him now. When he walks into a room, they all push their tongues down under their bottom lips and make mumbling noises. They take his books and they play Josh-in-the-Middle with them. When he tries to pick up a tray in the lunch queue, they all push him out of the way. When he complains that he has one of his headaches, they all volunteer to take him to the nurse. Instead they take him to the woods by the side of school and they leave him there, they make him find his own way back even though he isn't good at remembering routes or directions. He only knows his way home. They hunt him out at break-time and they ask him questions that make him scared: they ask him if he wants to sleep with them, they ask him if he has ever kissed someone. He gets upset and confused but he's been taught to be polite, so he always tries to answer them. Even when they hold his head near the toilet or dangle his books just out of his reach (which isn't difficult, right, guys, hahahaha), he's polite. He tries to laugh, he tries to understand the joke. He lets them get on with it.

And nobody stops them. Not even me. Because when I do, he gets angry with me. He tells me I've made it worse, I'm making it worse. Because Josh doesn't under=stand – to him, the world is simple, it has rules. Those kids have explained 'the rules' to him – don't tell, don't complain – and he really thinks if he plays his part, keeps his head down, everything will go away. He tells me not to stop them.

So I don't. I watch.

I hate myself.

SHE WALKS ON. The gun is warm in her hand but the blood in her veins is unbearably hot.

She feels nothing.

She has a list.

She made a list in the journal she has always kept. Scratching the names in the same way as Elijah (don't say his name his name can't be said his name his name his name) scratched words and pictures into his skin. She remembers the way the ink bled on the page and she bled and bled and bled too because this cut, this one, is too deep. There is no stopping what has begun.

She has made a list of the people who are responsible. A list she knows by heart. The people who have to pay. But now she is here, she doesn't see the distinction. *These people are all the same*, she tells herself. She has spent months online, months and years thinking about this, about how people put on pretty, popular faces to hide all the terrible darkness inside. She has spent months listening to anonymous people in chatrooms explaining this to her. Suddenly they all look the same – all she can think is *Bella Edward Bella* whenever she sees any of their terrified, perfect faces. She can't remember who has *actually* hurt her or Elijah, she just sees all the people who were there when it happened. And she can't control it; she can't stop herself from hurting them.

There is no stopping this thing she has begun.

At the end of the corridor she sees her teacher.

She raises her gun.

From the journal of Elise King, entry undated

Black-hearted people, empty faces
They hit you hard so they can feel
Shallow shells
Breaking things to hear them crack

You don't see me.
You won't see me.

I will break you. I will hear you crack.

Interview with Remy Dixon, 28th September, 2016

I was there when the first kids made it out.

I dunno, it was weird. It felt like we were standing there for years, man, all the police just standing around in the playground and all of us stuck behind the gates. But apparently it was only fourteen minutes from the first cop car showing up till they started getting ready to go in. I guess fourteen minutes doesn't sound like a long time, huh – and I know that what they was doing was important, they were trying to figure out how many shooters there was, and where all the kids would be, but most important they were waiting for *their* guns to show up. But yeah, it felt long, standing there.

Then, right, before they were even ready to get in there, we saw all these kids coming across the playground from the back of the building. That was a bit of a surprise, because we'd started seeing tweets and hearing people saying that all the doors were locked from inside. How twisted is that? The doors were chained up from the inside. And then suddenly you've got these kids, just running out with nobody stopping them.

Yeah, obviously all the police dived on them. It was like the kids kind of disappeared in all the black bulletproof vests. Then once they get to the gate they start popping back out again. Little kids bouncing around, crying and shouting stuff, that was weird, because everything felt really quiet before that, kinda like we were all holding our breath.

Then it all started to happen. There were ambulances and the yellow-coat police our side of the gate started pushing us out of the way, making space for them to open it. So many parents tried to get through the gap but they weren't having any of it, they were just letting the ambulances in and then the gates got bolted closed again.

I dunno, they said after that they kept the gates closed in case further attackers showed up. That makes sense to me. And people were going nuts our side of the fence, it was chaos. I reckon if they'd opened the gate properly, or if there'd been less police there, the crowd would've swarmed right in, all the way to the school. Bust those doors down themselves.

The police cars and the ambulances kind of made this shield, between the gates and the school, so Aish and me pushed through the crowd to get a better look through the fence. I saw kids from the year below, some of the Year 7s too. All crying and looking about like they didn't understand what'd happened to them. I saw one of the older kids had blood spattered on his school shirt.

We didn't see anyone we knew, nah. All the parents next to us were trying to get at the gates, trying to see if their kids were there, trying to get to them if they were. It was chaos. Insane. I felt sick. It was like we'd just jumped into something out of a film or off the news.

Aish had shown me this tweet about the shooter wearing a dragon hoody, and I knew then, I knew it was Elise, but I couldn't admit it to myself. I kept on watching through the railings, trying to see what was going on. I kept hearing the same Year 7 kid repeating the same thing over and over, even though nobody was listening to him. He was crying and he kept saying, 'She let us go, she let us go.' And I had to hold onto the fence because I felt like I was about to keel over.

And then this car comes screeching up the road, skids to a stop right outside. And a man jumps out of it and comes running right up to the gates. Elise's dad.

Yeah, that's when I knew for sure.

Extract from local newspaper, the Newton Post, *April 25th, 2013*

Missing schoolboy, Josh King, has tragically been found dead in woodland on the outskirts of town. It's thought he had been struck by a train while crossing tracks nearby. Detective Sergeant Kate Maize said in a statement today that officers were investigating reports that Josh was seen being chased by a group of teenagers in the area shortly before the incident.

Anyone with any information should contact Crimestoppers on 0800-555-1111.

From the journal of Elise King, entry dated 29th April, 2013

I can't. I just can't.

Interview with Julie Wu, 23rd September, 2016

The emergency operator told me to stay in the staffroom and wait for help. But even though I heard sirens at one point, nothing seemed to be happening. I don't know how long I had waited but Derran was losing consciousness again. There was supposed to be a first-aid kit in there but it was missing – things were always missing in that school.

The girl had died.

Briony, yes. She was a Year 11 student, though I'd never taught her. I covered her with my coat.

I knew I had to go for help. I didn't want to lose two students if I had a chance to save them. I put the phone next to Derran's ear, tucked under his cheek, and I told him he had to keep talking to the operator, that it was very important. He woke up a little then. He asked me not to leave.

I was afraid, of course. But I knew I had to do it. I went to the window and then I could see police making their way around the edges of the building.

I thought of smashing the window, because the windows above the ground floor don't open. But I did not want to draw attention to us, not when I was unsure where the shooter was.

I left the classroom and made my way down the hallway. I had closed the staffroom door but I hadn't locked it, though I didn't know if that was the right decision. I thought if police or paramedics got there before I was back, they would need to get in. I had to hope that the shooter would not return to that part of the building.

I reached the stairs. There was blood on the floor and some on the walls, a handprint where someone had slipped, I think. It was very, very quiet. I saw that the doors leading outside had been chained together from the inside. I turned left, towards the reception area. I hoped that there would be a first-aid kit there, or that I could make it to the nurse's office. I hoped that the police would be trying to enter there, and that I could ask them to send help for Derran.

There is a long section of hallway between the science area of the school and the reception. It has students' lockers along both walls, and two sets of bathrooms at either end. About halfway down, two girls were lying against the lockers. I did not need to look at them to know I could not help them. I tried not to cry. I tried to keep very quiet.

I think now that I should have just stayed in the staffroom when I saw the police from the window.

I think of myself walking down that hallway all the time. I see it in my nightmares. I see that figure appear at the end of the hallway, the gun half-raised, and I remember the way she pushed back her hood. I remember the way she looked at me. Like she was deciding. She walked towards me and her face was blank, so blank. And I was crying then, I was saying to her, 'Elise, stop, you must stop.' And I thought *This is it. I will die now.* But she kept that gun almost pointed at me as she walked on and on and then she had passed me. I turned around and I was still speaking, still saying her name. And I think, I know, that she heard me, I think she wanted to say something in return. But she kept her mouth pressed very tightly closed, like this, like she was afraid the words might escape. She shook her head at me, just once, like she was warning me, and her eyes were so full of fire, so angry. I have never seen someone look so angry before, it was like she was someone else entirely. I did not recognise the girl that I had taught.

She watched me right until she reached the end of the hall. I was leaning against a locker, I couldn't quite stand. I was shaking. She watched me and then she nodded, just a small nod, just enough for me to see. And then she was gone.

She let me live. I was one of the ones she allowed to live.

It was only when I reached reception that I realised she was heading back towards the science labs.

Interview with Gemma Morris, 27th September, 2016

I'd gone to school like normal that day. I woke up late that morning, because I'd been with Paul the night before, and I missed registration. I hadn't had time to charge my phone so I didn't get any of the messages from the others. So I didn't know about Elijah. I was totally in the dark.

Obviously I figured out something was wrong when none of the others were in first-period maths. I thought I'd have to go and beg a charger off the guy on reception at break-time so I could get hold of them, see what was going on. He always had loads of them, he was really cool about letting you take them even though we weren't meant to have our phones in school.

Yeah, people were still talking about the video of Eli and Elise shagging. Everyone knew I'd posted it, I hadn't bothered trying to hide it. So people kept asking me about it, laughing and stuff, and this guy Sean actually high-fived me. A couple of people were

236

giving me dirty looks, thinking I'd been out of order putting it up. But yeah, most people were acting like I was some kind of hero or something. It made me feel weird. Not guilty, exactly. Not then. But kind of uncomfortable. I'd pretty much decided I was gonna bunk off at break by the time I got to second-period chemistry.

We'd only been in the lesson five minutes when we heard the first shot. I guess nobody *really* thought that's what it was, not at first. Not round here. Mr Chambers just ignored it. But then we heard someone screaming, and then there was another bang, and everyone started looking around, getting a bit . . . not nervous, more like interested. Mr Chambers went to the window and looked out but he obviously didn't see anything because he just carried on with whatever he'd been saying.

But then there was the third bang, and that one sounded close, much closer, and then we heard people running, people yelling. We were on the first floor, where the corridor has a kind of balcony looking down over the entrance, and Mr Chambers went out and looked over. By this point, everyone was freaking out – people were out of their seats, looking out the window. And Mr Chambers came running back in, looking like he'd seen a ghost, and told us all to get under the tables. He turned off the lights in the classroom and then he went back out.

Nope, I'm fine.

Seriously, I'm fine. I can carry on.

They say he saved our lives doing that. I don't know, I guess they had some training or something, after one of the American school shootings, and I think Mr Chambers used to work in America too. He was one of the only ones who remembered to make us do that. Loads of the teachers just told the kids to run. We could hear them out there, all confused and yelling, and then we heard more shots.

Yeah, okay. Maybe we could take a break now.

WHEN HE HEARS the shots, his instinct is to run. He wants to curl into a ball or run as fast as he can back to that open bathroom window or just simply press himself against the wall and close his eyes and wait for it to be over.

He wishes he had his phone. He wishes he could call Aisha, ask her what to do. He feels a sudden need just to speak to her, to say anything, really – to hear her say anything back. Something to anchor him, to make all of this terrible, nonsensical stuff seem far away. She has always been able to do that, always been able to make it so that it's just the two of them, to shut everything else out. When he was a kid and he had night terrors, he'd wake to find her holding his hand, singing softly to him. She's the younger twin, by fourteen whole minutes, but she has always been the one who takes care of them both.

Elijah had night terrors too; that's one of the many secrets they have shared with each other. But though Ash's are a distant memory, a story his parents wheel out now and again – *Oh, Beta, you would scream and scream every night, we didn't sleep for five whole years* – he knows that to Elijah they are (were) a still-vivid experience, the scrabbling fear and the chest-crushing panic still as fresh as in those first couple of seconds after waking.

He has to carry on. He knows that. He's come this far; he has to keep going and try to make it stop.

He turns a corner in the corridor and finds a teacher there. They stare at each other, shell-shocked, neither sure what to do.

'You shouldn't be here, Ash,' Mr Chambers says, from his place on the floor. 'You need to get outside, to the police.'

'You're hurt, Sir,' Ash says, kneeling beside his chemistry teacher. Blood flows from a wound in his thigh, pooling on the beige vinyl floor. His face has turned grey and pale.

'It just nicked me,' Mr Chambers says. 'I'll be fine, Ash, honestly. Please. You go. Get out of here.'

But Ash doesn't move. He takes off his T-shirt and tears off one of its long sleeves and then the other. Awkwardly, delicately, he straightens out his teacher's leg and ties both strips of fabric tightly above the wound. 'It's an artery,' he says, head bowed over his work. 'You're bleeding to death.'

'I know,' Mr Chambers says quietly. 'Thank you, Ash, but please, you need to leave now. You can go and get help for me.'

'Help's coming,' Ash says, taking Mr Chambers' arm and slinging it over his own shoulder. 'Here, can you stand? Let me move you into a classroom. Somewhere more . . . hidden.'

He is surprisingly strong despite his wiriness, and Mr Chambers lets himself be lifted. The first classroom door they try is locked, though Ash can hear people whispering inside. He knocks, and then knocks again, impatient; calls out for help, and the noise inside goes instantly quiet. But nobody comes.

The next door opens; a caretaker's storage cupboard. Ash draws back but Mr Chambers stops him. 'This is fine, Ash – leave me here, I'll be fine here.'

'Sir—'

'Seriously. I mean it now, Ash. You need to go. Quickly.'

Mr Chambers shifts his weight away from Ash and stumbles over to lean on a shelf. He lowers himself to the ground, beside a mop and wheeled bucket. 'Close the door, Ash, and get moving. I'll see you outside, okay?'

Ash is frozen for a second. He doesn't think his makeshift tourniquet will be enough to stop the bleeding, not for long enough for the police to find his teacher. Unless Ash goes outside now and alerts them, or, better, takes Mr Chambers with him.

But then he hears another shot from upstairs. And he makes his choice.

'You need to lie down,' he tells Mr Chambers, pulling the rest of his T-shirt back over his head. 'Raise your leg against the shelf. Higher than your heart, at least. That will buy you time.'

'You get out there,' Mr Chambers says, 'and hopefully I won't need much time.'

Ash half-nods, turns away. He has never been able to successfully lie.

'Ash?' Mr Chambers narrows his eyes at him. His voice has become quieter. 'You're not going to do anything stupid, are you?'

Ash swallows. 'No, Sir. Not stupid.'

'Please get to safety, Ash. Let the professionals handle this. I don't want to see another life lost today.'

'Neither do I, Sir.'

Mr Chambers lifts his leg against the shelf with a groan of pain. 'Go,' he says, and Ash can't tell if this is implicit approval or his teacher turning a blind eye. As he closes the door, he hears another sentence, this one barely a whisper.

'I'm sorry about Elijah.'

He clicks the door shut, leaving Mr Chambers in darkness. He can't bring himself to reply.

From the journal of Elise King, entry dated 18th August, 2013

My room at Dad's is big and empty. He keeps telling me to unpack my stuff but I like it that way.

I haven't spoken to Mum since I got here. I don't want to talk to her ever. She calls and calls but she doesn't realise that I can't ever go back there. I can't even hear her voice because it reminds me. I know that she and Gareth are grieving too but I can't help them, and they can't help me. Just like none of us helped Josh.

Dad says once I start at school I'll feel better. I can 'move on', he says, as if you can ever get over the fact your brother was <u>murdered</u>.

But it is what I want. I want it to stop hurting. I want this huge hole in the middle of me to just not be there any more. I want a new face, a new feeling.

Today I dyed my hair. Black like ink. As far away from the old red, his old red. I put on make-up, more make-up than I ever wear. I lined my eyes and made them a different shape. I put pink on my lips like pretty is something I care about.

I look different. I look like one of them. And it helps.

Living with Dad is okay. He works a lot, and work's not something I'm supposed to ask him about. He owns a nightclub in London but I hear him talking on the phone sometimes, getting angry at people, talking about debts that are due or shipments coming in, whatever that means. I don't care – he leaves me alone and that's what I want. I heard him on the phone to Mum late at night last week – she called him, he'd never call her. He was yelling at her to leave me alone too, and I wanted to hug him.

Dad understands that we have to forget. It would be even better if we could just forget each other, too, and so we try and do that as much as we can.

But I can't forget about them. Olivia. Priti. Will. Their names run round and round my head when I lie awake at night, like they're scratched into my skin. I picture their stupid laughing faces, I imagine them chasing his little figure across the railway tracks. No CCTV, just one person's word, but I know. I <u>know</u> that's what happened.

And I let it.

*That's the part that I can't forget, no matter how hard
I try.*

Interview with Aisha Kapoor, 28th September, 2016

I'd only seen Elise's dad once before. He was out all the time and there were a lot of rumours about him round town, people said he was a drug dealer and a loan shark and stuff and that was why he was so rich and why their house was so big. But I don't know how much of that is true; people were kind of suspicious of rich people where we lived, and everyone loved to gossip, you know? We kind of ignored it really, we just thought everyone was jealous – and also it was quite convenient, him being away on business all the time, because it meant Elise had a free house. Sometimes when he was away she'd invite us over there for movie nights and stuff, and we'd watch horror films with all the curtains drawn and all the lights off. Remy and Eli would think it was funny to scare the rest of us; like Remy would sneak his arm down the back of the sofa and then stroke the back of your head in a super creepy way, that kind of thing. Once Eli left the window open so that the wind caught the curtain and it knocked a vase over at a really tense moment; my heart nearly stopped, I swear. Gem and me would always sit close together so we could hold hands and scream with each other.

No, Elise never really seemed scared to be honest. She always liked violent stuff. She liked gore and stuff, she thought it was all funny. People might think I'm making that up now, what with everything, but it's true. Her and the boys, they enjoyed it. Well, not Ash. He didn't mind blood but he didn't like to watch stuff that was violent for the sake of it. I mean, he played computer games and that kind of thing, but he always said they had a plot – he didn't like films that did stupid stuff for no reason, like when girls go into the basement after the murderer even though you'd obviously run out of the door at the first opportunity, do you know what I mean? Ash was always like that, he had to have logic even in stupid crappy films on Netflix.

Sorry, yeah. Elise's dad.

I almost didn't recognise him. He was all unshaven and sweaty-looking. He was wearing a suit like he usually did but with the shirt all creased and the top buttons undone. 'It's my daughter,' he kept saying, and that's when I noticed Remy was looking all pale and sick. The policewoman wasn't paying him much attention but then she had like a hundred parents all trying to get to their kids by then. But then he said, 'She took my gun,' and that's when she looked at him properly and took him past the ring of police and through the gates.

And I kept thinking *He can't mean Elise* but I guess really, deep down, I knew. I got hold of Remy's hand and he squeezed mine back so tight and I couldn't really breathe, just thinking about it all, thinking about everything that could be happening inside the school, about poor Elijah and about where Ash could be. There was this boy from our year, his name is Joshua, being looked after by the ambulance people. He was having glass or something taken out of some cuts on his face but all I could look at was the blood that was sprayed on his shirt. And I was still thinking, you know, *Not Elise*, like I couldn't connect these things I was seeing and hearing with her?

I couldn't . . . I just couldn't. I can't.

I'm sorry. It's just difficult to really imagine, you know? Even now.

Urgh. I . . . No, I'm okay. Just give me a second.

I still had hold of Remy's hand and I looked up at him, like I wanted him to tell me it wasn't happening. But he just looked back at me and I could feel him shaking. We knew it was true. We knew it was Elise.

That's when we started trying to get hold of Ash and Gemma again.

From the journal of Elise King, entry dated 25th September, 2013

I've started at my new school.

Surprisingly, I don't hate it.

People have been nice to me. A couple of girls asked me to sit with them at lunch yesterday. A couple of guys have offered to show me to lessons and stuff. I guess my new face is working. I'm painting over everything that happened. I paint flowers on my nails and wear tiny hoop earrings and I plait and twist my hair and sometimes I can pretend I'm just a girl who cares about nail flowers and hair plaits. Like that's all that's important.

I don't want friends. I don't need friends. I don't want people to be nice to me.

I want to forget.

I want to stop thinking the things I think when I'm alone at night. When I think about pulling Olivia or Priti along the ground by their hair, when I think about taking a knife and running it down their pretty perfect faces. When I think about taking a lighter and holding it against Will's face, or Orla's, when I think about pouring petrol over their clothes and letting them burn.

I still can't sleep. The thoughts fill me up and so I'm never tired. I spend all night looking at things on the internet. There are places where people understand me. There are people who hate the Olivias and the Orlas of the world too. I never knew these people were out there and it feels like such a relief that it's not just me who wants them to pay. Wants them all to get what they deserve. That makes me feel strong.

But then, in the morning, I want to forget again. I don't want to let this fire inside me keep burning because it will kill me. I want to keep on carrying on until it stops hurting me so much. I don't want to be this girl, I don't want to be the person who keeps finding themselves in the kitchen, looking at the block of knives. Touching them, stroking the blades. Dreaming.

He has a gun too. He thinks I don't know; he keeps it hidden. He's been going on about 'protection' since I got here – he tells me not to open the door if I don't know who's outside, he tells me I need to always carry something to protect myself when I go out. He gave me this thing, it's basically like a rock on a chain – he says if anyone tries to hurt me I should swing it round and hit them on the head with it. He gave me pepper spray too. I don't know who he's expecting to mug me in this crappy little town but maybe he knows more about everything that happened back in Newton than I realise. Maybe he's trying to help me.

I found his gun when I was looking for a pair of socks to borrow. He keeps it in his sock drawer which isn't exactly a sophisticated hiding place. I guess he doesn't think I'm the kind of kid to snoop around. He's wrong. He probably thinks I wouldn't know how to work it either – but he's wrong about that too. I wonder why he has it. I think he must be angry too. He must have dreams like I do.

I don't want to have the dreams any more. I don't want to stand in his room, holding the gun and wishing.

I want to forget. I want to stop pretending, I want to be a girl who cares about nail flowers and hair plaits again. I want to live and have friends and be okay. I want to stop hurting.

Interview with Zaira Rouhani, 29th September, 2016

She was always like that, Elise. Anyone who says different is a liar. I've seen so many people say how she was this sweet little kid who just got messed up because of what people did to her at our school. But that isn't true at all.

Well, yeah, of *course* it was a factor. The stuff the kids did to her and Josh was awful. I'm not going to deny that.

But how many people get bullied all over the country? Do any of *those* kids walk into their school and just start shooting people? No. That's not normal.

She was always angry. She was angry when her parents got divorced, she was angry when her mum met her stepdad. She'd get this, I don't know, flashes of it where her face would go all tight and she'd, like, bunch her hands into fists and just sort of, I don't know, vibrate with it. She learned to control it but I never wanted to be near her when she was in one of those moods. I once saw her throw her plate across the room just because her mum had burnt one of her fish fingers.

Oh don't get me wrong, she had loads of good things about her. Why else would we have stayed friends for so long? She was funny and generous and thoughtful. She'd always share her stuff and if you were upset she'd do nice things for you – give you sweets or let you borrow her DS or whatever. She was a kind kid. But she was angry. She was always angry.

I guess I do feel guilty, yeah. I can see how people might say we should have stuck by her when everyone was picking on her. But you know how it is, when you're a kid. You'll do anything to make sure it's not *you* who's getting picked on. If Elise had just sat and taken it, they would've got bored. But she couldn't, because she had that anger. She couldn't just sit down and take it. She never could.

Well, fine. You can think that if you want.

I'm just saying. She was an angry kid, and I was scared of her.

And it turns out, I was right to be.

THE SCIENCE LABS smell of ethanol, whiteboard markers, new carpet – fitted only a couple of weeks ago – and sweat. She has to be quick now. She can feel the shock of the thing wearing off, the people in the building and outside beginning to regroup, preparing to act. But her rage is not wearing off; if anything, it is gathering pace. She can feel it flowing through her and she feels free. Rage is erasing all of the other complex feelings she has been struggling with; its bright heat has wiped her clean inside and filled her full of fury. She understands this feeling, it is simple and it burns and it tells her that what she is doing is *right*. It is the only way. The fire will burn and burn and she will let it carry her until there is nothing left.

As she gets closer, she allows herself to think again about her list. Right now, the rage and the fire inside her are powered by the hate she feels for everyone here, everyoneeveryone. But now she knows that there are people in this building who are *truly* responsible. People who have truly done wrong, and who must pay.

She thinks of the moment she first saw the video of herself and Elijah. A totally private moment filmed in such bleak, naked footage, every flaw captured even through the phone's

254

blur. Her flesh pale and unappealing. Her movements clumsy. She thinks of the comments people left beneath it, the things they said about her. She thinks of what actually happened that night, although she doesn't want to. The way his skin felt against hers (*Cold*, she thinks although she's not sure that's true). The way she pressed her lips against his: hard, so hard, because she wanted so much to *feel* – feel something, feel anything but numb and afraid.

Well, now she does feel something. She feels it burn.

It's almost over now, she knows. The pain is almost over. Soon she will be free. But first the list.

She stops at a classroom door.

I'm coming for you, she thinks. *I'm going to take you with me.*

Interview with Gemma Morris, 27th September, 2016

What was what like? Hiding under the fucking table? Hearing shots and screams? What do *you* think?

Well, come on, seriously, babe. Ask a stupid question . . .

It was awful, okay? We had no idea what the hell was happening, we had no idea if we were safe up there or what. People were crying, people were whispering on their phones. I just kept listening. I could hear this banging, a different kind of banging to the gunshots, coming towards us. It took me a couple of seconds to release it was the lockers. Someone walking right down the corridor, banging the lockers. Like they were angry. Like they were letting us know they were coming.

Some of the boys were the first to go. Derran had gone out just after Mr Chambers and hadn't come back. Then Jake left, and some of the other basketball boys. I didn't know if that was a smart idea or a bad one. But then there was another shot, much closer to us, and people starting screaming. One of the girls, Tilly, started freaking out. She got up and picked up one of the stools and started hurling it at the window, trying to break it. I don't know what the hell she thought she was doing, we were on the second floor and those windows are like quadruple-glazed anyway, that was why we'd been sweating all spring.

All her mates got up and pulled her down and there was this kind of whispered panic as they tried to make her be quiet. But that was it, that made me lose it. I couldn't stay there. I couldn't just sit there without knowing what or who was coming.

So I got up. I walked right over to the door, and I creaked it open as quietly as I could. And then I just left.

It's kinda hard to describe to be honest. It was just the same old, normal corridor, except that right then, it was totally silent. I didn't realise I'd stopped breathing until I was almost choking on it.

Then I heard shouting coming from one of the labs at the other end of the hall, closer to the stairs. It was a girl's voice, and she was almost screaming, so I couldn't really hear the words. I just knew that something bad was happening in there.

But I also knew that I had to get out. And the only way out was past that room.

So I just went. I'm pretty quick when I want to be. I ran down the corridor, keeping my head right down so nobody would see me through the window in the classroom door.

I almost made it, you know.

I almost got out of there. Without looking back.

I don't know why I didn't. I don't know what made me stop.

Yeah, okay, I do. Honestly? It isn't like some people have said. It wasn't that I wanted to help the kids in that classroom. I wasn't being a hero or anything. I was almost halfway past the room, almost at the top of the stairs, when she started yelling at them again. I was close enough to hear the words that time. 'You all fucking deserve this,' is what she was saying, but that's not what made me stop. It was because I knew it was Elise's voice. I recognised Elise's voice.

And then I heard a shot. And before I knew it I was opening the classroom door.

From the journal of Elise King, entry dated 30th October, 2013

Something weird has happened.

I've accidentally made some friends.

It happened one Wednesday. This girl who sits in front of me in geography, Gemma, turned round and asked me for a pen. She's loud and pretty, the kind of person I usually avoid, and I waited to see if there was some kind of trick, if she was about to burst out laughing or if she was trying to distract me so that someone could stick something on my back or in my hair or steal my book or whatever. I'm used to that kind of thing, it's not easy to trick me. But after a second she was still just smiling at me, waiting. Like she actually did want a pen. So I gave her one and she said, 'So how are you liking the place?' and after that I couldn't shut her up.

To be honest, they actually seem nice. Gemma, and the twins Aisha and Ash, who are both really friendly and quiet and calm. I've spoken to Ash in maths before and you can just tell he's a good guy. Well, as much as you can ever tell that about a person I guess. Then there's Remy. I'm not so sure about him – he's loud, like Gemma, and he likes to tease people. It always seems like it's meant to be good-natured but making fun of people still hurts them, no matter how nicely you mean it. Plus he has this way of looking at me – at everyone – like he's trying to figure them out. He's always messing around in class, trying to get attention, which reminds me so much of the boys at my old school, the kind of boys who were always first to comment on photos of me or try and trip me in the canteen. But apparently he's been friends with Aisha and Ash since they were little kids, and they're so NOT like that that I'm starting to wonder if there's something more to him.

They ask me to hang out with them at breaks and lunch; Ash lent me a book he liked the other day. They're such little things and I had no idea I was missing them until I had them back. It felt like a punch in the heart when he gave me that book; when Gemma sent me a text to remind me that the new series of The Walking Dead *was starting.*

I'm not supposed to be doing this. I'm not supposed to be trusting people or letting my guard down, because that's how you get hurt. I don't want to care about anyone. I don't want anyone to care about me. I want to be numb.

But I sleep now. At night, I feel like I can sleep and sometimes I dream of things which don't end in blood or screams.

And during the day it feels so good to laugh and to talk about nothing much and to have company. Is that wrong? Is it a huge mistake? Will I make myself better or will I get hurt again?

Yesterday, Aisha was sitting in the canteen painting her nails, even though we aren't allowed to. It was Friday so I guess she didn't really care. It was a really pretty colour, this deep blue, and I said how much I liked it before I really realised I'd spoken. And she just smiled and held out her hand, like it was the most normal thing in the world, and because everyone was watching me, I gave her mine. She sat there and she painted my nails, carefully but not like she was uncomfortable, just like she didn't want to smudge my nails or hers. And I nearly cried because I realised nobody had held my hand or touched me, really, for a really long time. And it felt so nice.

When I'm sitting at the table with those guys, nobody else looks at me or stares or whispers, wondering why

I'm weird and a loner. I'm just normal, just part of a normal group.

And maybe that will protect me. As long as I'm careful.

Interview with Remy Dixon, 28th September, 2016

The police were inside the school twenty-three minutes after the first call. That's what they say anyways.

Doesn't sound like long, does it?

It felt like it.

It felt like years.

We could see them as they went round the buildings. They were creeping right up close to the walls, and they'd check through windows and doors and signal each time they found a room that was clear. Every time we didn't see that signal, we'd see them on their radios and we'd know there were people in there. Hurt or hiding.

The whole time, all I'm thinking about is Elise.

I dunno. I wanna sit here and say 'I just couldn't believe it', but I can't. Because I could. All of a sudden, I could picture her doing it. It was like I'd always known there was something off about her – I know that probably sounds like bullshit, like I'm just saying it cos of what happened. But I never really felt like we *knew* her, not properly. It always felt like she was holding something back. Sometimes I'd see her get this weird look on her face, like she was thinking really bad stuff. But then she'd just smile and be normal and every time I guess I just thought I'd imagined it.

I don't know. This kid from our tech class came running out with the bottom of his ear missing, blood pissing out onto his school sweatshirt, and I tried to make myself imagine her doing that to someone. And it was easier than I thought.

That's twisted, right?

Yeah. I'm fine.

Right, so we're there, at the gates, and Elise's dad is right in front of us, with a couple of official-looking people in suits and a couple of police officers, crying and crying. He just keeps saying it, saying: 'She took my gun'. Obviously that kind of blew my mind but I guess I shouldn't have been surprised – we'd all heard the rumours about him being some big don in London, about him having connections. My brother used to say he was a loan shark but I never knew what that meant, to be honest. But yeah, man, c'mon – you see the kind of car he was driving? And yet no one could say what he did for a job? That spells dodgy, course it does. So yeah, I'm not exactly shocked to hear he had a weapon; it's not like my dad or Ash's pulling out a gun.

Anyways then I see a guy in a suit standing close to the gate, with a load of officers sort of around him. He had a mobile next to his ear and he was looking around. Then this woman in proper body armour, like SAS-type stuff went up to him and started talking, pointing at bits of the school. Exits, I guess. I thought I saw her say 'locked' or 'chained' but again, maybe that's only cos of what I know now. She kept on pointing out certain windows or doors, and then at different groups of officers, and he was nodding, and I realised what was happening. They were ready to go in. Ready to go with their guns.

Yeah, I found out later that the nearest armed force was in Kings Lyme, that's like thirty miles away. They sent some from London, too, but they didn't get there till later. That's what took them so long to go in there, they were waiting to try and get as many guns as possible.

The rest of them had tasers. I tried not to picture Elise getting tasered. For some reason that made me feel sickest of all.

The whole crowd went quiet, watching them make their way across that playground. I think I forgot to breathe, to be honest. Aish was holding onto my arm so tight I thought her fingers were gonna go right through.

Nah, I couldn't watch. I kept on looking back at the kid with the bleeding half an ear, Miguel his name is, and the way his hands were shaking as he tried to find a number on his phone. I don't know why but that's the thing that sticks with me. The blood on his hands and on his shirt, the phone shaking.

And the hardest part was that we're all sitting there, wishing for it to be over. But obviously I knew then what that would probably mean.

I knew things weren't ever going to be the same.

From the journal of Elise King, entry dated 21st January, 2014

Everything has changed again.

A new boy arrived and Ash made friends with him, because he's Ash. The new boy's name is Elijah. He is tall and shy and always thinking.

He is Josh.

But he's so different too. He's uncomfortable with who he is but that means he's always watching people, assessing them, but not the way Remy does. He's afraid *of people, and that makes me like him. He doesn't automatically trust people, not like everyone else here. Not like Josh would have. It makes me feel safe with him.*

He's transferred here from Roehawk High, the place Maths Society went to for a tournament – that seems so long ago. It's not really close to my old school but it's somewhere I know and I feel like it means something. Like maybe I'm meant to protect him. Look after him. Maybe I can get it right this time.

He's so quiet it's hard to figure out what happened to him before. It was something, that's for sure. I can see it in the way he looks down all the time, the way he flinches when people are too loud around him. Something horrible happened to him. Which just makes me even more sure that he came here for a reason. Because I understand, I can understand. I can take care of him.

Maybe we can take care of each other.

Interview with Julie Wu, 23rd September, 2016

When I got to the reception desk, everything was silent. I didn't know what to do. I knew that I could get outside and get help there. I did not think she was going to come after me. But she was going towards the science labs and I knew there were still classes there, people hiding. I didn't know if I could just leave, if I should do something.

I went to the main doors and I tried to open them but they had been chained too. I could see all of the police cars and people outside and I tried to wave to get their attention but the glass in the doors is tinted and the way the sun was shining meant they could not see in.

The nurse's office is down a short corridor from reception and I knew that there was a fire exit beside it. If that was locked, I thought I could at least get some kind of supplies from the nurse's office, something that might help Derran.

It was very dark and very still and there are no windows in the corridor. I crept along and the whole time I was listening for any sound. It can only have been a minute or two from when she had passed me in the hall but it seemed like hours and because I had heard no shots I hoped it was over.

Then there was one. Muffled but I heard it. It went through my bones; I have never heard such a terrible sound. Often I think of that shot. It was a boy who I taught biology. I wonder if I had turned back, if I had tried to stop her, would he have lived? She might have killed me instead, and that would be far better than this guilt.

I almost turned back again then but by this time I had reached the nurse's office and I could see that the fire exit had not been locked. I don't know if she did not know it was there or if it had only been her intention to close off the main exits, to slow things down. I could see there were police officers coming closer now, some of them with guns, moving quickly around the building. I knew that they were looking for a way in.

I tried to open the door but the handle was stiff; it was jammed. It hadn't been used for some time, and with the hot weather the metal had swollen. I pushed at it with my whole weight and I began to panic. I'm not the kind of person to panic; I am usually very logical. But the fear had caught up with me and the sound of that shot had brought me to my senses. I kept on thinking of poor Derran alone in the teacher's lounge and of the children who were in that classroom where I had heard the shot. I kept on throwing my body at the door but I wasn't doing it properly; in my panic I wasn't pushing the handle down as I did so. My hands were shaking and I picked up a fire extinguisher from beside the door and I drove it into the glass with all the strength I had.

It took three goes and my hands were bleeding but then the first crack appeared. I hit it again and another appeared, this splintering sound that I will remember forever. I used all the power I could find, even though I was shaking so much I felt like I would fall. The glass splintered more – I found out later that it was special glass, designed not to smash – but I found that I could push the most damaged part and the rest buckled and then fell from its frame. My hands were bleeding very badly by then but I leaned out and I saw that the closest officers were coming towards me. I think that's when I started to cry.

They managed to open the door and then we were running across the playground, me and four or five officers and I suddenly was afraid that I would be shot, right there, from a window, when I was so close to getting away. And I was telling them 'The staff room, the science labs', trying to get their attention, trying to make sure they knew it was important. Trying to make sure they would all be saved, all those people still inside.

I don't remember much of the next few minutes but I know that I was put in an ambulance. I know there was a kind man who was tending to my hands and that a policewoman was sitting with me, trying to take my statement. I kept asking her to send people in to save Derran; I was sure that by then he would have died and she kept touching my arm and telling me that the police were inside the school, that it was all going to be okay. There were more shots then – I think two or three, I can't be sure. I pushed the paramedic away and went back onto the playground and I watched as they started running out, all of these children. I saw the police carrying out injured people. I waited and I prayed and I started to see faces I recognised, children from my classes.

It took a long time for them to get the paramedics inside, or at least it seemed to. Everything seemed to take forever and I was weak, almost fainting. The sun was beating down on all of us and I thought that I would be sick.

But finally they started bringing the gurneys out, people strapped on them, pale and bleeding. When I saw Derran I thought my legs would give way and I ran over and asked if he was okay. My police officer followed me and she guided me away, she moved me out of the paramedics' way. 'It's okay,' she kept saying to me. 'It's okay, you saved him.'

That was when I let her lead me back to the ambulance. I let them take me away from that place.

From the journal of Elise King, entry dated 8th May 2015

I can see things clearly again.

I was letting my guard down until Elijah arrived. I can see that now.

We talk about things. We understand each other and we <u>care</u> about each other. Everyone around us seems so small – all they care about is who's getting with who and who said what about who and it makes me want to scream. There are much bigger things in the world, terrible things happen to people all over the planet, and none of them can see it. They obsess about their little lives; they have no idea what real pain is. They need to be shown. NONE OF THEM CAN SEE IT.

Nobody except Elijah.

He's helped me to see how fake it all is; how shallow they all are. People like to tease him for his hair and now about his sister – how sick is that? He is good and pure and people try to hurt him, just like Josh. But he's different to Josh, because he sees them for what they are. He <u>gets</u> people, he sees the things they hide from each other.

It was him who told me that Aisha and Gemma were hanging out with those kids from the college. They've both changed – they both laugh at secret things and gossip about people who've done nothing wrong to them. They're shallow and self-obsessed and they never think about other people's feelings. But maybe they were always like that. Maybe I just didn't let myself see.

With Elijah, it's different. He has so many things to say about the world and art and life. He makes me realise that this tiny town isn't the end of everything; he reminds me that it doesn't matter what anyone thinks of me. They can't touch me; they can't hurt me any more.

But sometimes I want to hurt them.

Elijah has shown me how.

It started when they brought up his sister. They should never have done that. Nobody is supposed to know about that but me, I'm the only one who can be trusted with that. And to use it to hurt him . . . That just shows what scum people like Derran really are.

But I know something about Derran too. I know about him taking steroids; it's obvious if you know what to look for. At first I just wanted to shout it at him in a nice, crowded classroom, tell everyone the truth about their pathetic sports hero. But Elijah told me we could do it better. Anonymously. In a place where as many people as possible might see it.

And now the blog's up and running it's hard to stop. It's hard to stop telling these truths about people, it feels so good. So good to break down their false faces and show them for who they really are, all their flaws and their fakeness and their lies. To make them feel small for once. And the really great thing is that they all love gossip so much that they keep on doing the work for us, sharing the posts over and over again and laughing and whispering without realising that it could be them who we expose next.

It feels right. It feels like I'm doing something. Finally, I'm standing up to these people. To the Bellas and the Edwards (the Olivias, the Orlas, the Pritis and the Wills). I can tell all of my beta friends on 5-star that finally I am doing something. The revolution is beginning.

I'm so glad Elijah is here.

Extract from the journal of Elise King, undated

His skin is like silver
In the night light
His words are soft as silk
They keep me warm

Their words are glass
Bright and brittle and piercing
But he protects me
We protect each other
We build our secret world
We block them out

A better place

She closes the classroom door behind her; she isn't sure why.

'Stand up,' she says, the sound of her own voice harsh and unfamiliar in her ears. 'All of you, stand up!'

Nobody moves but she hears them, she hears them underneath the lab tables, crying and whispering.

'Stand up!' she shouts again, and she fires a shot at one of the benches, wood splintering and flying into the air.

The crying gets louder, but one by one heads begin to appear above the tables.

She's made a mistake; she's been sloppy. She moves into the room and the teacher, Mrs Olson, launches herself towards her from behind the supply cabinet. She reacts without thinking, finger already on the trigger, and Mrs Olson collapses to the floor, a clean, round wound in her forehead.

She returns her attention to the screaming, weeping class.

'You,' she says.

Sean looks back at her. He trembles, and when he blinks tears tumble down his cheeks. 'Elise, I—'

'Don't tell me you're sorry,' she says. 'Don't tell me you didn't mean the things you wrote. You were *laughing*. That video was private and you were laughing.'

And before he can reply, before she can think about it, she pulls the trigger.

The rest of the class scream and make for the door, panic twisting their faces into unrecognisable masks.

'Stop!' She fires the gun at the ceiling, freezing them in their tracks. 'Nobody's going anywhere! There are other people here on the list! Other people here need to pay!'

She scans the room anxiously but now she can't get their faces to line up, she can't remember who is most important.

In this crowd is Lucy Dinsdale, a girl who cares for her disabled mother, who once kissed Remy at a school disco and who has nursed a crush on him ever since, who often spends her lunch breaks helping shelve books in the library because the librarian is her neighbour and sometimes brings her casseroles and lasagnes to stock up their freezer. There is Jared Wilson, best long-jumper in the county, who gave evidence against his brother in a drink-driving trial last year, and whose parents haven't spoken to him since. Fariz Ahmet, Gemma's sort-of ex-boyfriend, who likes to ride off-road motorbikes in the woods on the outskirts of town but who once left her a voicemail singing her an Ed Sheeran song, and Honey Thomas, his sort-of current girlfriend, who once wet herself in a school assembly because her favourite author was there to give a talk.

And there is – there was – Sean Scott, who was only predicted five A–Cs in his exams next month; who was yet, despite his many stories to the contrary, to lose his virginity; who once climbed onto the roof of a neighbour's house to rescue a tangled kite from a TV antenna for a crying little boy on the pavement below. Sean who hated his ginger hair and worried about

278

his skinny arms and relentlessly teased friends and strangers because it made him feel better.

But she no longer remembers their stories; their voices are a rush of white noise that roars in her ears and hides the steady thump of her heart.

'You!' she shouts, trying to concentrate. 'All of you!'

The door clicks open behind her. 'Oh leave them alone, Elise.' The voice low and calm, a tinge of impatience even. She wheels around, sweat running down her back, and Gemma gives her customary greeting: a rise of her eyebrow.

'You,' Elise says. '*You.*'

Interview with Gemma Morris, 27th September, 2016

I can't remember what I said to her. My heart was beating so fast I couldn't really think. She turned round and I saw Sean behind her, this kid from my maths class. I could tell it was him because he had this crazy curly hair, really bright ginger. He was facedown on his desk and there was blood around his head. It sounds weird, but it felt like time had slowed down, like I had time to think about how Sean had shared the video of Elise and Elijah all over his Facebook and Twitter. I saw the gun in Elise's hand and I just tried not to look at it.

'What the hell are you doing?' I asked her. I honestly felt like I was in a dream.

She had this totally weird look in her eyes. They were glazed over, like she was kind of out of it. But when I said that she got really angry.

'This is all your fault,' she said, and that's when she lifted her hand so she was pointing the gun at me.

I didn't know what she was talking about. I didn't know about Elijah then. But I said 'I'm sorry' anyway. I said it a couple of times, anything to try and stop her from pointing that thing at me.

She wasn't listening. She kept getting closer to me, and I remember looking at the gun and thinking *Why doesn't she just do it?* She was a couple of feet away and she said, 'You killed him.'

Then I heard this voice behind me say, 'No, she didn't.'

I turned around and it was Ash. He didn't even look at me, he just kept his eyes on Elise. He had a hand out to her, like she was a dog he was trying to get to stay or sit or something.

'This won't bring him back,' he said to her, and her face sort of creased for a second, like she was going to cry. 'I loved him too,' he said, really quietly, but she wasn't listening any more. She was looking at me.

'You have to pay,' she said. 'People like you—'

Sorry. I just need some water. I—

Nope, I'm fine.

Okay.

She said, 'People like you are poison. You shouldn't be allowed to live. You're toxic.' Something like that. It's hard to remember now; it happened pretty fast.

And I said I was sorry again, I was crying, and I said I was sorry and I asked her – I begged her – to let me live. I couldn't move. The whole time that gun was pointed right at me and I couldn't stop looking

281

at it. I could see her finger right there on the fucking trigger.

'Close your eyes,' she said. 'It'll only take a second. This is best for everyone.'

And I did.

It happened at exactly the same time: the bang of the gun and his hands on me, pushing me away.

And then I was falling. It felt like I was falling forever.

From the journal of Elise King, entry dated 13th May, 2015

I think I have done something bad.

I was angry. I feel angry all the time now and it scares me. These big sudden waves of it sneak up on me and then crash down and I can't do anything except be carried away on them. I want to break things and hurt people and scream and scream. The only thing that can calm me down when I feel that way is Elijah.

But today Elijah wasn't around.

I don't suppose she even knew she'd done it. Aisha can be like that sometimes, totally oblivious. She was just walking along, heading for our normal table in the canteen, and there were these two boys picking on another boy. He was huddled over with his backpack on and they'd opened it without him knowing. They were laughing and throwing one of his books back and forth when Aisha got in their way. The book hit the floor at her feet and all three boys turned to look at her.

It's not even like she didn't see what was happening. She picked it up and glanced at the boy with the backpack and then she just THREW THE BOOK BACK TO ONE OF THE BULLIES. AND SHE <u>LAUGHED</u>.

I had to get up and leave. I felt sick. By then one of the teachers had seen what was happening, and gave the kid his book back. He didn't even seem upset. But that's NOT THE POINT.

I can't take it, I can't take it.

All those things I left behind, they keep on bubbling up. The memories are unstoppable; I feel their fingers on my skin, I hear them laughing. I see those pictures of me online, all the comments piling up underneath, ping ping ping, people talking about how ugly I am, how pathetic. I look in the mirror and I try to see my new face, the new me I built, the new me who doesn't care, but all I see is him. Josh.

The worst part is that Elijah is sinking too. I can see it on his face. He hates the world: how cruel it is, how much pain there is. He doesn't have anger to carry him like I do. He goes inwards instead, locked up tight where nobody can get to him.

Something happened between us. I don't know how, or why. I just wanted to help him. I wanted to feel close to him, and I think he wanted that too. We got drunk and we kissed and . . . things went too far. I don't think he liked it. He's been avoiding me ever since. He spends all his time with Ash instead.

And so when I was feeling so angry today, I didn't call him. I didn't try and stop the waves; I rode them. I posted something I shouldn't. The secret I shared was Aisha's but even now I still feel like she deserved it. I don't know I don't know I don't know.

I'm going to call him now. He'll make everything okay again.

He moves quickly along the corridor because he can hear her voice, both of their voices. He pleads and prays in silence and then, when he reaches the door, he steps into the room.

'You killed him,' she spits at Gemma, her usually pale face a blotchy purple, her voice hoarse and raw.

'No, she didn't,' he says, and he's surprised, once it's out, at how steady his voice is.

Elise looks at him, her face twisting like he's betrayed her. 'She *did*,' she says. 'You know she did. The video—'

Gemma starts to cry. 'What are you talking about? Did something – is Elijah okay? Elise, I'm sorry about the video, I was angry . . .'

'Shut *up*,' Elise says, her voice low and poisonous now, darting through the air like a snake striking. Her eyes are still on Ash.

All the fear has melted away now; he feels calm, he feels distant, as if he's watching all of them from somewhere very far away. He keeps his eyes locked on hers, as if by doing that he can keep her as still as he is.

'Elise,' he says, choosing his words as carefully as he always does, trying each one on for size in his head. Sometimes sentences take hours to spill out of him, but not this one. This one comes too easily. 'This won't bring him back.'

He has chosen wrong; once these words are out, their truth is undeniable. And finally, finally, he has to accept what has happened, he has to let the knowledge that Elijah is gone find its wings and take flight. The impact of it makes him weak at the knees and the next words slip out unchecked. 'I loved him too.'

He sees the words sink in. He sees her face, which had begun to soften into something unbearably sad, harden again. She turns away from him.

'This is your fault,' she tells Gemma. 'You have to pay for this.'

But still she doesn't do it. She doesn't move. There is just the gun, held out in front of her, her hand trembling so slightly that only Ash can see the way her finger twitches towards the trigger. The tiniest of movements, it takes his breath away. Gemma looks back at her, tear tracks through her make-up, the skin underneath weirdly vulnerable.

'People like you are poisonous,' Elise says, patiently, as if she's explaining something to a child. 'This is better for everyone.'

And then, in a flicker of pity: 'Close your eyes. It'll be quick.'

Ash has never been fast; he has never been agile. His reflexes are quick when it comes to action on a screen, but in real life he's always dropped anything he's been thrown, always tripped where there's something to trip over. But when her finger closes over the trigger, he sees things in slow motion. He sees his own hands reach out, he feels his whole body launch towards Gemma. He hears the shot. He sees her go flying to her left, sees her head hit the edge of the table and her body flop to the floor, unconscious. He sees the world turn sideways as he continues on his own trajectory to the floor and he sees – with such painstaking detail that he wishes he was able to close his eyes – Elise turn the gun on herself.

But it isn't until he is lying on the classroom floor, his ears still ringing with the echoing shots, that he feels the pain in his chest. Feels the blood leaking out, hot, hotter than he's ever imagined, pulsing as it leaves the bullet wound just above his left pectoral muscle.

It isn't until he's lying there, looking at the crumpled figures of his two friends, listening to the chaos of the classroom around him and the thunder of footsteps from the hallway beyond, that he feels the life leaking out of him.

Interview with Aisha Kapoor, 28th September, 2016

It was so crazy. More and more ambulances were showing up, and TV cameras, and we were being pushed and pulled as everyone tried to get to the gates, all these parents trying to get to their kids and everyone crying and yelling. We'd watched the police get ready to ram down the main doors and then we'd seen Miss Wu smash her way out of the fire exit – that was when everything started happening, fast. The police went running into the school, guns raised, and there were so many of them, so, so many, they just kept coming.

All I could think about then was the six of us on the beach, and the way Elise looked in the moonlight. Her face always had this kind of secret quality to it, do you know what I mean? Like there was a lot going on under the surface but that she'd never let out. I was watching all of this stuff unfold in the playground and all I kept thinking was how much I wished I'd tried to find out, to get to know her.

No. I couldn't hate her. Not then.

There was a police officer standing near us and we could hear his radio crackling and people talking over it. He was, like, leaning his head close to it so he could hear over all the noise and he went over and started talking quietly to Elise's dad. He put a hand on his arm and looked down as he was talking. Elise's dad kept on crying and shaking his head.

'She shot herself,' Remy said, and he showed me his phone. Someone had tweeted it, this girl who was in the classroom when it happened. I don't understand what she was thinking. Like, if you live through that, the first thing you do is go on Twitter? When people you went to school with are right there, dead on the floor?

No I'm okay. I just want to get to the end of it.

The police were helping all of the kids out of the school, and letting the paramedics in. There were people pushing everywhere, students pressing up against the gates to hug their parents, cameras flashing everywhere, and then the stretchers started coming out. The paramedics were running across the playground, wheeling them towards the ambulances. The first one came close to the gate and I saw that it was Mr Chambers. He was really pale but he was alive. I didn't know then, obviously; I didn't know it was Ash who'd helped him. I didn't know.

Another gurney came out and it was Derran – he didn't look good and my stomach dropped, you know? Like when you're going to be sick except worse. I could see a third person being wheeled out but someone pushed in front of me then, crying, and for a second I couldn't see. Remy was tall enough though, and I looked up and I saw him see who was on the stretcher and I saw his face go pale.

'Who is it?' I said, even though I didn't want to know. 'Remy, who is it?'

'Don't look,' he told me, as the woman in front moved out of the way and I could see again. He was crying. 'Close your eyes. Don't look.'

THEY SIT IN the waiting room without speaking. Aisha beside her huddled parents, Remy with his head resting against the wall, face tipped up to the ceiling. The space between each tick of the clock seems to stretch out and the silence expands and presses down on them. Outside the waiting room, people hurry past, blue-gowned and urgent, their faces hidden behind sterile white masks.

Later, Gemma will join them, the cut on her head from where she fell against the lab table neatly stitched. She knocked herself unconscious and she's still feeling woozy; sitting next to Remy, she keeps repeating the same sentence in a dreamy, disbelieving whisper. *He saved me*. Police officers come and go, asking questions, but Mrs Kapoor screams at them until they leave. And in the end, there are other witnesses, so many witnesses, that the things the three of them say or think matter very little. After the first hour, they turn off their phones, the notifications and the messages and the calls silenced.

Journalists gather outside the hospital, outside their houses, the crowds of them outside the school swelling and then slowly dispersing as the story develops. But in the waiting room, it's just them, just waiting.

Remy thinks of all the things that could have happened differently: if he and Gemma had never gone round to Elijah's that night, if Elijah and Elise had never started their blog, if it had been him and not Ash who had been smart enough to break into the school to try to stop Elise. If Elise had never arrived at the school, if Elijah hadn't. He thinks of the six of them on that camping trip in Newquay. He thinks of all the times he sat on Ash's bed playing computer games, of the way Ash's long, elegant hands look on the controller, his thumbs moving frantically but precisely over the buttons. He thinks of the way Ash's books are neatly lined up on the shelves, grouped by subject, author, sometimes size. He closes his eyes and wills his friend to live.

Gemma can't stop remembering the way Elise looked at her, the cold, calm hatred in her face. The things she said about Gemma, about how toxic she is. She tries to forget, tries to think of something else, but all her mind can produce is Eli. Eli with his head bent over his book, his hair falling in his eyes. Eli smiling shyly at her. Eli inking patterns onto his arms. She knows now what has happened, what Eli has done, and her brain keeps trying to show her that too. She stops saying how Ash saved her. She starts wondering why.

With her hand locked in her mother's, Aisha tries not to think, just to wish. People have always asked her if it's true that twins have a psychic connection, if she and Ash ever think the same thoughts or feel each other's pain. She used to laugh and say no, but now she feels as though her pulse is his; if she can just keep her heart beating, he will have to live. She bunches her other hand into a fist and concentrates as hard as she can and she tries to imagine her brother waking up. *Open your eyes*, she thinks, again and again. Finally the surgeon returns to the waiting room and tells them that they can see Ash now.

'The operation went as well as we could have hoped,' he tells her father, who starts weeping again while her mother remains stoically, mesmerisingly silent. As they walk down the too-bright corridor, she wills Ash to wake up even harder; she pictures him sitting up in bed, waiting for them.

But he isn't awake; he is very still, an oxygen mask covering his face. He looks too slim in the bed, his skin greyish. They enter the room carefully, they are very quiet. The machines around him beep a constant rhythm which she starts to find comforting. She sits in the chair beside his bed and holds his hand and watches his face and waits.

As the minutes drift by, she listens to the electronic sounds of Ash living, and she starts to wonder what things will be like in a month, six months, a year's time. She starts to wonder how each of them will tell this story, how each of them will see their part. Who each of them will blame, the details that each of them will think were important. They will each have a different starting point, she realises, a moment where they think it began. They used to be a group, but now each of them will have a separate history, a different version of this terrible thing which happened and which split them apart. There will be so many ways to tell it she wonders if they'll ever really know where it started, if it could have been stopped.

And then her grip on Ash's hand tightens, and she watches as his eyelids flicker, once, twice – and then begin to open.

Acknowledgements

A big thank-you to the many people who supported me, in various ways, during the writing of this book.

To Cathryn Summerhayes, Siobhan O'Neill and all at WME and Curtis Brown for championing, chasing and reassuring.

To Emma Matthewson, Monique Meledje, Tina Mories and all at Hot Key Books, for making it a wonderful place for my books to be.

To Ian Ellard and Joey Connolly, for putting up with me.

To Hayley Richardson, for being the alpha beta.

And to Margaret, Richard and Daniel Cloke, for everything.

Nicci Cloke

Nicci Cloke is a full-time writer, part-time doer of random jobs. These jobs have included Christmas Elf, cocktail waitress and childminder. She is also the organiser and host of Speakeasy, the only London literary salon to host regular YA events. She published her first novel for young adults FOLLOW ME BACK in 2016 with Hot Key Books. Her first adult novel SOMEDAY FIND ME was published by Fourth Estate in 2012 and her second LAY ME DOWN was published by Cape in 2014. Follow Nicci on Twitter: @niccicloke.

HAVE YOU READ NICCI CLOKE'S GRIPPING FIRST BOOK?

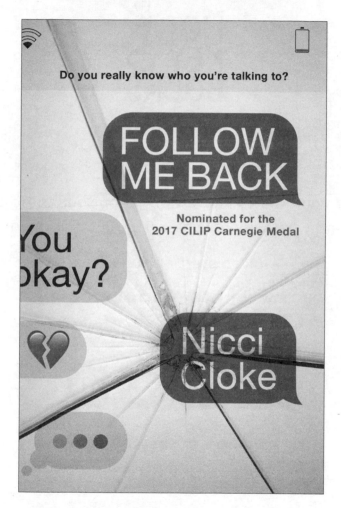

OUT NOW IN PAPERBACK AND E-BOOK

HOT
KEY
BOOKS

Thank you for choosing a Hot Key book.

If you want to know more about our authors
and what we publish, you can find us online.

You can start at our website
www.hotkeybooks.com

And you can also find us on:

We hope to see you soon!